HANNA

OMEGAS OF ECHO FALLS
BOOK 1

M.P. STARKWEATHER

Acknowledgments

I would like to thank:

My Bunnies and Sisterwives, who encourage me to keep writing, even when it's hard;

My amazing PA, Gwen, who is my twinsie;

My Alpha Team who tries hard to keep me on track;

My Editing Team who does their best to make sure my books make sense and have as few typos as possible;

My Cover Artist, who's responsible for the gorgeous images on the front of this book

and My ARC Team, who catch some of the things the rest of us miss.

I want to dedicate this book to my Bunnies. You know who you are, and this series would not be possible without you. I'd also like to recognize my two biggest fans, my husband Josh and my son Thom, who will probably never read any of my books. Thanks for pushing me to chase my dream. I love you both to the moon and back.

Contents

Prologue: There Is No Pack

TEN YEARS AGO

REMY

"Dad, I don't understand. Why don't you want me to talk to Mr. Evans? You know how I feel about her. And the boys feel the same. We're ready to claim her now." My voice is strained as my eyes meet my father's.

"Son, you're an alpha. When you and your brothers get mated, you'll be the head alpha. There are responsibilities that come with that. You have to be ready for a life-long commitment when you take that step," he insists. I understand his point, but I don't want to wait. I want Hanna Evans to be ours now.

"Then what do I need to do? Because we're not going to change our minds. The three of us are ready." I ask, desperate to figure this out and get my life sorted.

"Are you? And is she?" He shakes his head, then continues. "If you're set on this path, talk to Evans. See what he says. Without a clear plan of how you'll take care of his daughter and your pack, he's not gonna agree. Rem, I love you, but you're just not ready for this," he says softly.

"You'll see, Dad. I can do this," I insist. Walking out the door with my head held high, I make my way to the bakery. I need to do this now, before I lose my nerve.

I see Hanna's dad at the counter, waiting on customers. The bakery isn't too busy right now, so it may be the perfect time for this.

"Mr. Evans, could I speak to you in private?" I ask when I step up to the counter. His smile falters for a second, but he recovers quickly.

"Sure, Remy. Let me get Amber to cover the front for me, and we can talk in the back office," he says, walking away to ask his wife to deal with the counter while we talk. A few minutes later, I'm standing across from him in a small office behind the kitchen. My hands shake and sweat drips down my back.

"What did you want to talk about, Remy? Is everything okay with your dad?" he asks. From his expression, I think he knows exactly what I'm here for, even if he pretends not to understand. I take a deep breath, willing my nerves to calm.

"Well, sir, I want permission to court Hanna. My brothers and I are completely in love with her, and we want to make a pack and family with her. Since I just graduated, I felt like it was time," I blurt. There are definitely more tactful ways to approach this, but an eighteen-year-old alpha with very little life experience wouldn't understand that yet.

"No." That one word destroys me.

"No? I'm sorry, sir, what?" I ask, dumbfounded. Of all the ways I saw this going in my mind, Mr. Evans saying no was never one of them.

"Look, Remy, I understand that you boys care about Hanna. I just don't think you can take care of her the way she deserves. And this is a big commitment. Claiming an Omega isn't like marrying a beta. There's no going back if things get hard. You have to be completely sure. And I'm not sure that you guys are the right ones to take care of my girl. How are you going to take care of her? How would you provide for her? I know you don't want to work at the steel plant," he says.

And he's right. She deserves everything, and I have nothing. This won't work. I need to make something of myself first. "Mr. Evans, would you reconsider? Is there anything I can do to convince you?" I ask, my fists clenching at my sides.

"If you boys can show me that you're serious, maybe. But I need more than you just coming here without a plan of action. Do you understand?"

I nod, my brain reeling at his words. I have to find a way to support and take care of Hanna. I walk out of the bakery feeling lost and alone. I don't know what I can do to prove to him that I love his daughter and want her to be mine. No, I don't want her; I need her. Hanna Evans will be mine. I just have to figure out how to make it happen.

HANNA

I'd been so sure that Remy was going to talk to Daddy this week about us. Of course, he didn't tell me that, but he's been acting nervous. I haven't seen him since two days after graduation. He has to be coming up with some grand gesture to show me that Daddy's accepted him. That has to be it, right?

I can't handle waiting anymore, so I stop by their house on my way to the bakery. Remy's car is gone, but Leo is sitting on the porch, his dark hair falling nearly over his golden eyes. Maybe he'll know what's going on with his brother. He stands when he sees me. I jog up the walk and throw my arms around him. Leo hugs me back, but I can tell he's hesitating.

"What's wrong?" I ask, tilting my head to meet his eyes. "Where's Remy?"

"Remy left. He went to Chicago," Leo says. Tears fill his eyes, and I don't understand what he's saying.

"Chicago? Why?" I ask, confused. He'd never mentioned that particular city before. "When will he be back?"

"Apparently, he wants to be a world class chef, and that's where he has to go to do it," Leo responds, his arms still around me. "I don't know if he is coming back."

"You mean, he's not gonna ask my dad?" My own tears threaten to fall, and I duck my head, stepping out of Leo's embrace. If Remy's gone, pack law will keep us from being together. For an Omega, it's all or nothing. I know that because I've read every bit of the law, trying to understand what needs to happen for me to be claimed by the Kerrisk boys.

Leo shakes his head. "I'm sorry, buttercup. Will and I aren't giving up, though. We'll fix this."

"I have to go," I whisper, turning and racing home. My world is crumbling around me. I can't breathe and my chest aches. He left. Remy left, and he didn't even care enough to say goodbye. I can't let myself believe that Will and Leo can figure out a way to fix this. Without Remy, there is no pack. The laws are clear. And so is the message Remy sent by leaving the way he did.

When I get home, I lock myself in my room, falling face first onto my bed as the tears blur my vision. The most painful part of this situation is that Remy left without saying goodbye. Why would he do that? What made him change his mind about me? What did I do wrong?

one

Back in Town

HANNA

"Hanna! Are you ignoring me?" my step-sister Julie's voice breaks through the trance I was in. Setting the muffin tin on the counter, I open the oven, place it inside, and set the timer before I turn to face her.

I shake my head. "Sorry, Jules, what did you say?"

"I asked if you saw that Remy Kerrisk is back in town. I guess his dad left him The Diner, and he's come home to run it," she says with a wink.

"Well, that would explain why business is down. People are probably trying to help them out, since Rob's gone," I suggest. "The town did the same thing when their grand-dad passed away and left Leo the bar." Her groan of frustration nearly makes me laugh.

"That's not why I asked, and you know it. Stop playing coy and admit that you still have a crush on him!" Julie is nothing if not persistent.

"Jules, I haven't seen him in nearly ten years. What we had wasn't exactly a crush, but that's a fair question. I couldn't say for sure if I would react the same way to him now or not. I mean, his brothers are cute enough, sure," I admit.

"So, that means y'all can finally get together, since Remy is back," she insists.

I don't have the energy to argue with her about my love life right now. We may not be busy, but I have work to do. A quick glance at my watch tells me that I have one shot to get out of this line of questioning. "Don't you have to work today?"

Her eyes go wide and she looks at her own watch. "Shit, I'm late. Sheriff's gonna kill me." As the only daytime dispatcher for our town, Julie is under a lot of pressure to be on time and good at her job. I hand her a to-go cup of coffee and a sack of muffins.

"Share the muffins, and I bet Conley'll forgive you," I offer, shoving her toward the door. As soon as the door clicks shut behind her, I sigh. I know she means well, but I can't focus on my gossip-obsessed step-sister's theories about my romantic involvements or lack thereof right now.

I need to find a way to bring business back to the bakery. Which is why I'm here earlier than usual on a Saturday morning. I'm testing out some new recipes. With the last batch of muffins in the oven, I can start on the cookies before I move on to the new donut flavors.

And if I want to open on time, I need to get moving. Stopping to chat with Jules nearly derailed my morning. I love her, but that girl has always been the gossip queen. Even if I was ready to admit that I still have a thing for the Kerrisk boys, Jules is the last person I would tell. Don't get me wrong, she's not malicious about it; she just doesn't know how to shut up. The girls and I have often joked about how telling Jules was the best way to get information spread around town.

Once I have the baking done, I prepare to open the shop. Evans' Bakery was my father's dream, and when he died, Mom let me take over. My sister, Amanda, and my brother, Blake, help me out most days. When they're not available, other people in town drop in and lend a hand. It's one of the things I love most about living in Echo Falls. The majority of people here are considerate and helpful. It's rare for someone to leave and not come back. There's a sense of community here that I've never heard of anywhere else. It's not like I've ever left, though, so I can't say what's happening outside of our town limits.

That thought reminds me of Remy's return. Ugh, the last thing I want to think about is Remy Kerrisk. We'd been teenagers, flirting and, I'd thought, planning to start dating when he suddenly left town to pursue his dream of becoming a chef. I don't blame him for leaving; I'm pissed that he didn't bother to tell me his plans or even say goodbye. I'd thought he and his brothers were going to ask my dad for permission to court me; the first step toward claiming and becoming a pack of our own. Turns out, I was wrong.

Pack dynamics have prevented me from dating his brothers. Around here, it's all or nothing. Since Remy left, his brothers haven't been able to date anyone. We still hang out, just never alone, and we have to be careful about any kind of affection. I don't agree with it, but I can't fight Pack law.

I'm sure that Julie was hinting at that earlier when she suggested that I still have a thing for Remy. Of course, I do. But I'm so mad at him that I don't want to admit it. Hell, if the man walked in here and proposed, I'd be hard pressed to turn him down. But I'll be damned if I'll admit that to anyone right now. He owes me an explanation and a whole lot of apology.

It's been almost ten years, and I can't seem to turn those feelings off. I'm not sure I'll ever be able to trust him again, though. And trust is important. Since Dad died and Mrs. Patton ran off with some out-of-towner young enough to be one of her kids, I've watched Mom and Mr. Patton develop a level of trust I can only wish for with another person.

They've been together for years now, and he's good to our family. I can't help thinking how hard all of this has been on him, since his wife lied, cheated, and stole from him before she dropped signed divorce papers on his doorstep and ran off. They were the talk of the town for a while, and it got pretty bad. Mr. Patton, I'm supposed to call him George, almost lost his construction company. I shake that thought away, not wanting to get lost in the past right now.

I'm relieved that Amanda and Blake are available this morning, so I don't have to be out front waiting on customers. It gives me time to focus on baking and coming up with an idea to bring business back. It's not completely dead in here this morning, which is great. But it is a lot slower than usual. I peek out front to find my brother deep cleaning parts of the seating area, since at least half of the room is empty.

My heart jumps when I see all three Kerrisk boys walk through the door together. Okay, boys isn't a fair term. They are clearly men, and hot ones at that. Remy's golden-brown curls and piercing blue eyes are just as stunning as I remember. I duck back into the kitchen before they see me, listening at the door. I can't help it; I'm almost as nosey as Julie.

"All I'm saying is that you should back off with all the changes at The Diner," Leo says. Oh, wow; I didn't realize that they were fighting about the changes that threaten to put me out of business.

"I don't understand why you want to push the bakery out. Everything here is so good," Will insists. It's so sweet how they both seem to be on my side. As much as I don't want to cause family problems for them, I love that they care so much. If only there was a way for me to be with them and not their annoying oldest brother.

I can't make out Remy's response, but from the frustrated huff, I hope they're not about to fight. "Look, bro, just try something. Get a muffin and a coffee. Have a conversation with her before you kill her business, okay?" Leo's quiet words barely make it to me through the swinging door. I don't wait to hear his brother's response, turning back to my kitchen and forcing myself to focus on my work.

REMY

If this asshole doesn't stop telling everyone that I'm trying to put Evans' Bakery out of business, he's gonna kill my dreams before I ever have a chance to try for them. And just to be clear, destroying Hanna Evans' business or dreams has never been my goal. I'm certain that I won't be able to convince her of that, though.

Nope, my plans definitely don't include alienating the gorgeous baker. I'd hoped to catch a glimpse of her, all that dark hair wrapped up in a bun on top of her head, her green eyes blazing with her anger. Even furious at me, she's the most gorgeous Omega I've ever seen.

But that's obviously not gonna happen today. If I know Hanna, she's hiding on the other side of the kitchen door, listening to every word we're saying. Which is why I'm keeping my voice low enough that my asshole brothers can barely hear me. I wish Leo could take a hint. This isn't a conversation to have here. Not now.

I need Leo and Will to shut up. No one has to tell me how talented Hanna is. I already know, and if I have my way, we'll get a lot closer. It's been nine years, ten months, and twenty-six days since I walked away from this place. Since I walked away from her.

Part of me thought I'd never come back. Of course, my heart knew better. No matter how hard I try, I can't escape this place. Hell, as much as I hate small-town life, I knew I'd come back sooner or later. I had to. My heart is tied to this town, and always has been.

Hanna is here. She's all that matters. It's gonna be hard to make her see it, but I left for her. I mean, not completely for her; I guess *for us* is a better way to put it. I needed to prove to myself that I could be what she needs. She deserves the world, and I plan to give it to her. I just have to convince her that she can trust me and make her forgive me first.

Since she's avoiding me, that's gonna be harder than I'd thought. Of all the reactions I'd expected from her to my new dessert and breakfast menus at The Diner, hiding wasn't one of them. I spend every day waiting for her to come in and destroy me over it. The only reason I made the changes I have is to goad her into confronting me. It would have taken the old Hanna two days to show up at my door and ream me over it. I won't admit how many times I've imagined her stomping into the diner and giving me hell over everything I've done to hurt and annoy her. Yet I'm still waiting.

I guess we've all grown up and changed since I left. Maybe she doesn't care anymore. I can't believe how badly I've fucked this up. I have to find a way to fix it without my brothers stepping in or me being forced to admit to her why I did all this. There's no point in coming across like an immature dick when that wasn't my intent. I just wanted to remind Hanna how much heat there was between us before I left.

What if she's moved on? Is there someone else? Fuck. A low growl escapes me, and I look up to find Hanna's sister Mandi staring at me. "Uh, hey, Remy. Can I get you something?" The look on her face—the fear in her eyes—causes me to clench my jaw.

"Salted caramel mocha and a coffee-cake muffin, please. And my idiot brother is buying," I say, gesturing to Leo. He doesn't even argue with me over it, just pulls out his wallet and finishes giving Mandi his order combined with Will's. I take the offered coffee and muffin, nod my thanks, and turn to leave. Fighting with Leo in the bakery is not going to fix this. I have to talk to Mayor Barry before she announces the Founder's Day festivities.

I have a plan to put in motion. Convincing Hanna that she's still in love with me won't be easy, but it's gonna start with making sure she has to spend a lot of time around me for the next month. Glancing over my shoulder, I notice that Will and Leo aren't following me. Good. I slip out the door and head toward the courthouse. Hopefully I can be in and out before they realize what I'm doing.

LEO

I pretend not to notice when Remy ducks out the door of the bakery. After paying for breakfast and leaving a large tip, I turn to Will. "You wanna do me a favor and see if you can figure out what he's doing? I gotta talk to Hanna and make sure she's okay," I say, turning back toward the kitchen and stepping away from the dining area.

"I'm on it," my little brother says, rushing to catch up to our older brother without being seen. He'll fill me in later, and I'll catch him up on what Hanna says. We work well together as a team.

I nod to Blake as I pass him with my coffee and pastry, heading into the kitchen as if I belong there. It's not unusual for me to drop in and visit Hanna, and we keep things strictly hands off because of Pack laws. It's not what I want, but I can't afford to be exiled.

"Buttercup? You okay?" I ask once the door swings shut behind me. The look on her face when she turns around is enough to have me setting my breakfast down and crossing the room to pull her into my arms. There's no law against hugs and comforting a friend. "It's okay, buttercup, he's gone. I can keep him out of here if you want."

She shakes her head, turning to bury her face in my chest. Her dark hair is in a messy bun on top of her head. I rest my cheek on the soft tresses and rub my hand up and down her back, enjoying her maple cinnamon scent as it mingles with the smells of the baked goods. I hate that my brother still has the ability to make her cry like this, even after ten fucking years. I have half a mind to beat the shit out of him for it. On the other hand, I know that this intimate contact will have her scent on me for the rest of the day, and I love it.

"I'm okay, Leo, really. He just caught me off guard. And I heard part of what you guys were saying about him trying to run me out of business. Thank you for defending me," she says quietly.

"It's nothing, buttercup. I can't stand the way he's acting since he came back. Something is going on with him, but he won't talk about it. All he says is that he has a plan, and we need to trust him. I can't trust someone who ran off without an explanation," I admit. I know that it hurt Hanna more than it did me or Will, because at least Remy told us goodbye.

"I don't want to come between you and your brother," Hanna says with a sniffle. She's still hiding her face in my shirt.

"You aren't. And you won't," I insist, lifting her chin so she has to meet my eyes. Our faces are so close that if I shift slightly, I could kiss her. My eyes dip to her pouty pink lips, mesmerized as her tongue darts out to moisten them. "Hanna, I promised you almost ten years ago that I'll fix this. I meant it. With Remy back, it'll be easier to do. If you still want us," I add. If she's changed her mind, then there's no reason to keep trying to mend things between them.

"Of course, that's what I want. It's all I've ever wanted. I just don't think he feels the same way we do," she responds. The doubt in her eyes destroys me. I press my lips to her forehead before dropping my arms from around her.

"You know how he is," I say, hoping that I can convince them both that this could work out the way we all wanted. "I've gotta get to the firehouse, but I'll text you when I have a break. Okay?"

Hanna's smile lights up the room, and I know that I won't have to worry about Remy upsetting her anymore today. "Sounds good." She leans up and kisses my cheek, then I turn and grab my breakfast. I don't even care that it's cold now.

HANNA

I watch Leo as he picks up his coffee and pastry, then walks out the kitchen door without another word. It's so hard to let him go without kissing him the way I want, but we both know how this works. A stolen kiss here and there is fine, but not in public and not during work hours. Anyone could have come in while he was holding me, and we'd both have been in trouble. His sweet amaretto scent is so calming, as is his Beta nature. Knowing that his scent will remain on me until I shower later is comforting.

Living in a small town is great, but we don't need the gossip mill going nuts about us breaking Pack laws. I take a moment after Leo leaves to calm myself down. I can't keep letting Remy get to me this way. At some point, we're going to have to talk like civilized adults. I'm not sure how that's gonna work, though. He's avoided me for nearly a decade. I'm not even sure he's actually an adult. Running away like he did was childish, and coming back only to avoid and ignore me is even more immature. Could he say the same about me? Maybe, but I'm not the one who ran. I've been here the whole time.

With the way it's getting harder and harder to resist giving in to my desires for Will and Leo, I know that Remy and I are going to have to talk. And it should be soon. I know it won't be long until my heat hits, and I'd really rather not go through another one on my own.

WILL

As much as I wanted to see Hanna this morning, I don't argue when Leo asks me to follow Remy. Sometimes being the little brother sucks, especially when I'm an Alpha, and have had my life figured out since I was sixteen. My oldest brother gets special privilege because he's the oldest Alpha. Personally, I think that little bit of power went to his head. He needs to get his shit together so we can officially claim Hanna. Leo and I are tired of suffering because Remy can't man up.

Doesn't matter, I remind myself. Hanna needs Leo's calming Beta presence right now, and I have to figure out what the fuck Remy is doing. It takes me a few minutes to find his scent after I leave the bakery. I follow it toward the courthouse.

Why would he be going there? I slow down when his scent gets stronger, ducking around the side of the building when I catch sight of him. Waiting a minute, I walk inside behind a couple who are chatting about applying for a permit for something. I let them block me from my brother's view as I watch him. When he enters the mayor's office, I stop in the middle of the hall.

After waiting a beat, I make my way to the closed office door and peer inside through the small window at the top of the door. I can't get any closer without risking him seeing me. All I can do now is wait to see how long he's in there and where he goes once he's done. I wait almost an hour, then decide to head out. I have clients after all, and since I work by myself, I can't just expect someone else to take over for me.

As I leave the courthouse and head to my shop, I shoot a quick text to Leo to let him know that I haven't found anything out.

TWO

This Is New

REMY

By the time I walk into Mayor Barry's office, I'm half convinced that one of my brothers is following me. I can't let that stop me from following through on my plan. If I want Hanna to forgive me and accept us as her pack, I need to convince the mayor to help me. I've known Joy Barry since I was five years old, and she came in to talk to our kindergarten class about being a lawyer for career day.

She watched my brothers and I grow up, and we watched her political career advance until she made it to her goal. As her secretary escorts me into her office and shuts the door, I take in the appearance of the woman standing in front of me. Mayor Barry is a Beta in her mid-sixties, with salt and pepper hair that's coiled into a bun. She's attractive for an older woman, reminding me of my grandmother.

"Remington Kerrisk! To what do I owe this pleasure?" she exclaims when she sees me. I blush at her use of my given name, taking the hand she offers.

"Mayor, it's lovely to see you. I had something I wanted to discuss with you about the Founder's Day competition this year. If you have a moment, I would love to explain further. I could use your help," I admit with a sheepish grin.

"Color me intrigued. What could you possibly need from me? I can't rig the contest, even for my favorite young man," she says with a smile, gesturing for me to take a seat.

Am I really going to confess my feelings to this woman and ask her to help me win Hanna? Yes, I am. And I hope that she agrees to my plan.

"Thank you. I have to start by admitting that this is about a girl," I say.

Joy's eyes light up, and she smiles. "Hanna Evans. I take it she hasn't forgiven you for running off? I can't say that I blame her, sweetheart."

"I know. And I deserve her anger. But my brothers and I love her, and we want her to be ours. I'm certain she feels the same way. I just can't get her to talk to me."

"But you have a plan, and need my help," she says.

I nod. "Yes. In the past, the Founder's Day competition has always been a baking contest. I assume that remains the same this year?"

"Of course," she answers, motioning for me to continue.

"I would really appreciate it if you grouped the teams for activities prior to the contest. Window decoration, making and hanging flyers, things like that. But group opposing teams together for those things," I say.

Her eyes go wide, and she nods. "And you'd like me to pair your team with hers, so she has no choice but to talk to you. I can see how you think this might work. What if she doesn't sign up?"

"I'll make sure that she does. Honestly, I've done everything I can to get her to confront me since I've been home. And before you ask, yes, I did try going to her to talk. She refused to answer the door, calling through it to send me away." I hate admitting that, but if I want Joy's help, I have to be honest with her.

"Is that why you've changed the menu at the Diner?" she asks.

I nod, closing my eyes for a moment. "I expected her to come at me for it, not hide and pout. I even went in the bakery this morning to talk to her, but my idiot brothers were with me and wouldn't shut up long enough for me to corner her."

"I hate that you kids are suffering like this. Everyone in town knows how much you all care for each other. It's been hard on your brothers and Hanna since you left. You know Pack law as well as I do. It broke my heart to have to keep them apart," she admits.

"Does that mean you'll help me?" I ask, locking my eyes on hers.

HANNA

I run down the sidewalk to the American Legion building. Fuck. Fuck. Fuck. I can't believe I lost track of time, and I'm late. Today should be the announcement for the Founder's Day contest, and I'm going to be the asshole walking into the Town Meeting late. I stop outside the door, giving myself a second to catch my breath, before I open it and walk inside.

Several people turn to look at me when I enter. I want to turn around and run back to the bakery or just melt into the floor. I hate being late, and being the center of attention is even worse. Well, it's too late now. I'm here. Mayor Barry pauses when she sees me, smiling kindly at me while I find a seat. I take the only open one near the back, not paying attention to who it's next to.

"As I was saying, this year we will be mixing things up a bit. Our baking contest will be a team event as usual. However, this year, we will be pairing up teams to participate in all the events leading up to the contest itself. Sign-ups will be open for one week, starting today. Once sign-ups close, I will pair up the teams and let everyone know who they'll be working with."

Wait, what? Murmurs flow through the crowd at the announcement.

"That sounds like it could be fun," a familiar voice next to me whispers. Shit. How did I not realize that I was sitting right next to the one person I've been avoiding?

I hum, non-committal, refusing to turn my attention on him. I will not look at Remy Kerrisk. I will not fall back into our familiarity. I make these vows to myself even as I try to get a glimpse of him in my peripheral vision. What are the chances I'll get paired up with him? Surely, there are enough groups who will sign up that I won't have to deal with him any more than absolutely necessary.

I push that thought out of my mind, along with the memories that threaten to overwhelm me. Besides, I can always talk to Karen and convince her to get Mayor Barry to pair me with someone other than Remy. It's not like the whole town has no idea of what happened between us. She has to understand my reluctance to interact with him.

I do my best to ignore him as the mayor explains the rules of the competition and details the changes. I'm not thrilled at the possibility of being stuck in close proximity with him, but

I can't give up on the idea of the prize money, either. I need that money if I'm going to keep the bakery open.

I'll do whatever it takes. I just hope that doesn't mean working with Remy to organize, decorate, or advertise the contest. I don't think my heart could take being around him. He's impossible for me to resist. Once the meeting is over, I can't get out of there fast enough.

Unsure if I'm surprised Remy didn't try to stop me from running away, or disappointed that he didn't attempt more conversation, I race home from the meeting.

WILL

I take a swig of my beer, considering my brother's question. "Of course, he's up to something. I just don't know how we can figure it out. Why can't we ask him directly?"

Leo scoffs, wiping the bar. "Because he won't tell us. You know that as well as I do. Remy doesn't share his plans with anyone until he decides it's time for them to know. That's why we're in this situation now. The asshole decided it would be better to run away than to talk to us."

I drink more of my beer, thinking back to when our oldest brother ran off almost ten years ago. He barely took the time to say goodbye to us, and apparently didn't bother with letting

Hanna know he was leaving. All because Hanna's dad told him we weren't ready to court her.

If he'd stopped for two fucking seconds, he might have realized that Evans was right. When he asked for permission, Remy was barely eighteen, Leo was seventeen, and I was fifteen. Hell, Leo and I were still in high school. What kind of father would agree to giving his daughter to a pack that young with no real financial security? But no, hot-headed Remington Theodore Kerrisk cannot be bothered to stop and think about the logic behind an argument that doesn't involve him getting what he wants, when he wants it.

"Fuck him. We should petition the Council to kick him from the pack. Then we could court Hanna ourselves and not have to wait for him to agree," I say, slamming my beer bottle down. I realize in that moment that I've let my Alpha nature take over and I'm acting at least a little bit like my oldest brother. Lucky for me, Leo is a steadfast and patient Beta.

"You don't mean that. And even if we could, they'd just dissolve the pack and make things that much harder. The Council isn't gonna just hand you control when I'm older. I can't do it because I'm not an Alpha. We need to corner him and talk about this," Leo insists.

I know he's right, but it's hard to admit that we actually need Remy. He didn't just run out on Hanna after all. He left us too. And we had to deal with everything when Gramps died, then when Dad passed. If Mama hadn't moved to Texas with Aunt Juliet, we'd be the ones taking care of her, too.

Instead, we handle Leo's Place, The Diner, and Kerrisk Carpentry. Or we did, until Remy came back to claim The Diner as his inheritance. It's not like Leo or I wanted it anyway. But things haven't been easy for us, and Remy doesn't seem to care. He's so self-centered and grumpy since he came back. Part of me wants him to leave again. I can't admit that, because if he did, I'd feel guilty.

I'm surprised that Hanna has waited all this time for us. Love is strong, but it isn't always enough to sustain people through something like this. Don't get me wrong, I'm glad she hasn't moved on. But someone as amazing as her could have any pack she wanted. And for some reason, she wants us. It makes me want to work harder to be the man she deserves.

"Look, I know he's being a dick. We have to make him talk to us tonight. I can't call a pack meeting, but you and I can approach him together and force the issue," Leo suggests.

I nod. "Okay. I'll wait to pound him until after we talk," I agree.

LEO

I stall Will until Jasper comes in to relieve me, then drive us home. We live close enough to walk, but I never take the chance that one of my friends will need a ride when I don't have my truck. Once we're home, all we can do is wait for Remy to grace us with his presence.

It's ridiculous that we feel so much animosity toward him, but he brought it on himself. The asshole made life-altering decisions for us without so much as a word of warning until it had all been decided. I can't blame Will for being pissed and wanting to exile him. If it wouldn't fuck us over completely, I would go along with it. I did so much research when Remy left us, I could probably be the mayor.

There are no ways around Pack law, though, so we're stuck. And since we need our older brother, we're going to sit him down and talk about this. Like fucking adults. Or I'm going to knock their heads together.

Remy surprises us by showing up half an hour after we get home. "Oh, hey, guys. I brought dinner." He sets take-out containers on the counter before turning the oven on. "I'll get everything heated up. Then we need to talk."

Well, this is new. Big brother wants to talk to us. I wonder if he's planning on letting us in on his top-secret plans. I know he has them. Remy always has a plan.

"We can talk while you get stuff ready, if that's okay," I say, moving from the doorway to the kitchen island. I gesture for Will to follow. When we're both seated, he and I stare at Remy, waiting for a response.

"Oh, sure. Was there something you guys needed? I'll explain mine while we eat," he insists. Of course, he doesn't want to tell us what's up. It doesn't matter. We'll get it out of him, one way or another.

"We need to talk about Hanna," I say, not giving Will a chance to respond first. I don't need this to start as a fight.

"What about her? Do you want to accuse me of killing her business again?" he retorts with a scoff.

"Rem, look, I know you aren't trying to put her out of business. But that's what's happening. You have to know that," Will says, his hands clenched into fists on the counter.

"Don't worry about it. I have a plan," he says. See? Remy always has a plan. It's annoying.

"Bro, just listen. If we have any chance of courting her, we need to discuss this and agree on an approach. She's still open to the idea, but if you don't get your shit together, that could change," I say. I know my words are harsh, but it seems to get his attention.

"Did she tell you that?" he asks.

"What? That she's interested? Yeah. That she's going to move on if you can't work this out? No, but she really didn't have to. It's obvious," I answer.

"I swear, if you fuck this up for us, I will run you out of this town," Will threatens. I hold up a hand to stop them before things escalate.

HANNA

"Wait, you sat next to him at the meeting and didn't even talk?" Rissa asks, her eyes going wide.

Next to her, Maisy chokes on her sweet tea. "Are you okay, Mais?" I ask, trying to change the subject. My besties won't allow it, though.

"Don't change the subject," Maisy coughs. "How could you be that close to him and not talk?" I roll my eyes, wishing I hadn't bothered to tell them about the mayor's announcement.

"Can we talk about something besides Remy, please? I can't deal with it right now. I need to figure out how I'm going to win this contest. Y'all need to help me. Please," I beg. I glance from Rissa to Mais and back. They exchange a look, then nod.

"Okay, we'll drop it for now. But we are going to talk about this soon. You need to figure out if you can forgive him so they know if y'all can court or not. I'm sure Leo and Will are ready to force the issue," Maisy says, her tone suddenly serious.

"Understood. I promise, I'm thinking about all of it. I just can't right now. It's all too much," I answer.

"We need to figure out what kind of treat you're going to make, then," Rissa insists.

Maisy nods. "Grams is making her award-winning German chocolate cookies." Oh, shit. Those are the best cookies I've ever had. I don't know how I'll compete with that.

"What can I possibly make that could compete with Grams' cookies? There's no way for me to win this, especially with *him* competing," I whine. Rissa rubs her hand down my back and Maisy takes my hand.

"That's not true. You can't give up yet. What if you make those delicious mocha muffins? Or an orange cranberry cake?

There are so many amazing things at the bakery that you could do," Mais counters.

She's right. It's not fair for me to give up before I've even tried.

THREE

Power Struggle

HANNA

Waiting to find out who my team is paired with has been the hardest part of this competition so far. Mayor Barry closed sign ups a week ago and should have emailed or called by now. I know I'm driving Mandi and Blake crazy stressing over it.

"Seriously, Han, if you mention the contest one more time..." Blake says, rolling his eyes. "It's not gonna matter who we get teamed up with for the extra stuff. The only important thing is that we have the winning recipe. It's not like Remy can force you to do anything you don't want to. He's not that kind of guy." I know my brother is right, but that doesn't mean I want to be forced to spend time with the man who ran away from me a decade ago. My heart can't take it.

"I'm sorry. I'll drop it, I promise. Not one more word about it from me." I turn back to the mocha muffins, pulling them from the oven when I see that they're done. "We need to narrow down our recipe options, though, and settle on which one is best."

"You can't go wrong with the mocha," a way too familiar voice says from the doorway.

I jump, nearly dropping the tray of muffins. "What are you doing here, Remy?" He shouldn't be in my kitchen. My heart shouldn't race at the idea that I like the way he looks standing in my kitchen in his fancy chef's coat with his name embroidered on the chest.

"Mayor Barry asked me to deliver your team pairing in person," he says, holding out an envelope to me. I carefully set the tray of muffins down and cross the kitchen to take the letter from him.

"Why didn't she just email it?" I ask, tearing the envelope open and reading the note. Fuck. This cannot be happening.

"Well, she knows we have history. She probably thought you'd take the news better coming from me than her. I really can't say for sure," he says. I hate how nonchalant he's being about this whole thing. It's as if being near me has no effect on him at all. I fight to hide my reaction, though I'm certain he already knows how I feel about it.

"I see. Well, we're a little busy here, so if you don't mind," I trail off and turn away from him. Remy grabs my arm to stop me from walking away. Fresh citrus scent tickles my nose, and I barely hold back my sigh.

Blake locks eyes with me for a second, then runs off like a chicken shit. I'm not sure if he's giving Remy time to win me over or allowing me to destroy the man who broke my heart.

"I do mind, Hanna. And I think you know that. I understand that you're mad at me, and you don't want to talk right now. But we're going to be working together to prepare for the Founders' Day festival. So, can we set our issues aside and focus on that for now?" His words are quiet, and I almost believe that he means them. But I don't know if I can trust him.

"I don't think I can, Remy. Being around you is too much. I'll call Mayor Barry and ask if we can switch partners. It's not fair for you to be stuck with me, when I can't handle being around you," I say, holding my head high.

"You think this is easy for me, cupcake? It's not." He lets go of my arm, crossing his over his chest. "I'm dying inside, knowing that I hurt you. I get that you don't trust me, and you can't believe me. Just give me a chance to show you that I mean it. Unless you're too scared," he says. I can tell that he's pissed, which is a relief. If he'd said all those things to me with any other look on his face, I might have broken. But knowing that he's pissed makes it easier to deny what I'm feeling.

"You make everything look easy, Remy," I say. "Leaving, coming back, destroying my business. It all comes easy to you.

Especially walking away. That was the easiest thing you've ever done, wasn't it? Don't pretend that you still care about me. I'm sure the mayor will take pity on our situation and reassign our partners. Now I have to ask you to leave so I can get back to work."

I'm shaking, and I don't know if it's rage or hurt. All I know is that I need him to leave. I can't be this close to Remy without either punching him or kissing him. And right now, my fists are itching to take a swing. My cheeks heat, and tears burn my eyes.

"I'll go for now. But you're not getting rid of me that easily, cupcake." He steps closer, pulling me into his arms. With his lips a whisper away from mine, he says, "You still love me, and you know that I've always loved you. I will make you admit it."

The move catches me off guard, and I don't even have the ability to growl at him to let me go. For a moment, I think he's going to kiss me. Instead, he presses his lips to my forehead, then drops his arms and walks away. I'm left standing in my kitchen, unable to process what just happened.

I'm not sure how long I stand there, staring after him. Blake comes back into the kitchen and waves a hand in front of my face. "Are you okay?" he asks.

I nod slowly, trying to decide if I'm lying to my brother or not. "What's up?"

"I called Mayor Barry for you, while you and Remy were...uh...talking. She won't change the team pairings. I have no idea why she's being so stubborn about it, but she refused to even consider it. I'm sorry, sis." Blake wraps his arms around me, hugging me tightly. "It looks like we're stuck with him."

Well, fuck. I guess there's nothing I can do about it, if Mayor Barry refuses to consider changing it. "We'll just have to make the best of it, I guess. We can't drop out of the contest; we need the prize money too badly. And you'll be here the whole time, right?" I pull back and look at my brother.

"I won't leave you alone with him if I can help it. And Mandi will be here too," he replies.

"Okay, let's get to work, then." I do my best to ignore the tug in my chest at the lingering citrus scent.

LEO

Just when I start to beat Henry at Mortal Kombat, Jasper yells from the kitchen. "Chef is here and he doesn't look happy." Henry smirks at the way Jasper refers to my brother by his job title, but I know it's meant to be a sign of respect. Jasper has worked in professional kitchens before, and he's one of very few people who actually seem to like Remy. I don't understand it.

We turn off the game as my brother stomps into the building. "I've got this," I say, leaving Henry to meet him in the dining area. "What's wrong?"

"I don't know if this plan is going to work. I just came from letting Hanna know that our teams are paired for the

Founders' Day activities. She's seriously pissed and insists that she's going to call the mayor," he says with a growl.

"Take a breath. It can't be that bad," I insist. I consider for a minute what Remy told me and Will about his master plan to win Hanna over. I warned him it was a bad idea, but he refused to listen. Now he's seeing that I may have been right.

"It is. She tried to pretend that she wasn't mad, but she was basically vibrating with the effort it took not to hit me. What can I do? She won't listen to me; she's made it clear she's not interested in being in the same room as me. This whole thing was a bad idea. What was I thinking coming back here?" he rants.

Well, shit. I wanted him to be humbled by her reaction, not defeated. "Rem, come on. Let's talk this through. You have to give her time to accept that she'll be spending time with you. Did you at least tell her that Will and I are on your team?"

He shakes his head. "She all but kicked me out as soon as she read Mayor Barry's note."

"I'll call her. Trust me, this will be okay. I know I wasn't a fan of your idea in the first place, but it's too late to back out now. You've already convinced the mayor to go along with it. We'll have to knuckle down and make it work," I argue.

"Do you think she'll talk to you?" he asks. It's clear from his reaction that he has no idea how close Will and I are with Hanna. Should I tell him or just let it be? I'm gonna think it over for a while first.

I take out my phone and push the button to call Hanna. Honestly, I don't know if she'll talk to me since he upset her so badly. But I have to try. A grin spreads across my face when she answers on the second ring.

"Hi, Leo. What's up?" Hanna's voice is velvety smooth. She doesn't sound upset at all. I wonder if it's because I'm calling, or if she wasn't as mad as Remy said.

"I just found out that we're teaming up for Founders' Day stuff leading up to the baking competition. I know that you're probably not thrilled about spending so much time with Remy, but wanted to make sure you know that Will and I are on the team, too," I say, not bothering with small talk.

She lets out an audible breath. "He told you that he came to see me?"

"Yeah. He's pretty upset. Says you got mad and threw him out."

"I did. I can't do this, Leo. I can't pretend like everything is okay and hang out with him like old times. It's too hard," she says quietly.

"What's she saying?" Remy asks in a hushed whisper. I shake my head at him and focus on Hanna. She needs me right now.

"It's gonna be okay, buttercup. I promise. I won't let him harass you too much. I can't keep him from talking to you, especially since we're gonna have to work together," I pause, listening to her rant about how infuriating Remy is.

"He just walked in here like he owns the place and started telling me how this was gonna go. The asshole didn't even apologize or try to explain about him leaving without a word. It was like he thinks he did nothing wrong. He thinks I can just go back to the way things were back and pretend like the last ten years never happened. I can't do it. There is no way I can work with him after everything he's done. I can't, Leo. I won't." Her anger is palpable through the line, even while her voice shakes with hurt.

"I understand. But you're not going to let that push you out of the contest, right?" I scrub a hand down my face, hoping that Remy hasn't ruined this for us.

"No, of course not. I can't back down. But I'm not giving in; I can't. I have to go now, Leo. I'll text you later, okay?" she says, barely waiting for me to agree before she hangs up.

"Well?" Remy asks when I drop the phone into my pocket.

"She's pissed all right. But she's not giving up. You're gonna have to work really hard to win her over. It's not gonna be easy, big bro. You really fucked this up," I explain.

"You and Will are going to help me with her, right?" he asks. I've never seen Remy so unsure of himself before. He's always been confident to the point of cockiness, even when he's wrong.

"Of course, we will. But we can't force her to spend time alone with you," I insist.

"I understand. I just need to figure out what approach to take. I'll win her over. You'll see," he says, a smile crossing his face as he turns to leave. What the fuck am I going to do with him?

WILL

I see Remy's car at the firehouse when I walk by, so I turn the opposite direction, heading back toward the bakery. I was going to see if Leo wanted to go out to lunch since things in town have been dead, but I'm not dealing with our oldest brother right now. Instead, I'll treat myself to a cup of coffee and something sweet. If I'm lucky, I'll get a minute alone with Hanna.

Pulling open the door to Evans' Bakery, I see Blake manning the counter. He smiles at me and nods toward the kitchen. "She probably needs a hug; your asshole brother was here earlier," he says as I walk past him and push open the swinging door.

"Thanks, man."

The moment I see her; I know that her brother wasn't exaggerating. She looks like someone on the verge of a breakdown. "Hey there, sweet pea. I heard you could use a hug?"

When she turns and our eyes meet, I see the unshed tears in hers. Wrapping my arms around her, I take in a deep breath of her maple cinnamon scent. It mixes with the baked goods and my mouth waters. I focus on pushing a little of my sandalwood cedar scent at her, hoping it calms her a bit. I know her well enough to realize that Remy didn't just hurt her when he stopped by, he pissed her off and she's struggling to get her emotions under control.

"You wanna talk about it? Or should I just go find Remy and beat his ass?" I ask, holding her close.

"Oh, I would love to see that, but I'm okay, really. I think it upset me more that he was the one who told me about being paired up with you guys for the festivities. I'll get through it." I love how determined she sounds right now, even though she's clearly upset.

"I'm proud of you," I say, watching as her eyes go wide when she leans back to look at me.

"What? Why?" she asks.

"Because I know you didn't back down and you're not giving up. You could have let him intimidate you, but you didn't." Before I can talk myself out of it, I lean over and press my lips to hers in a gentle kiss. I want more, but we both know that it can't happen right now. Pack law is clear, and unless we'r e officially courting, we're not permitted any intimacy. I could get us both in trouble for holding her this way. I definitely shouldn't be kissing her at all.

Hanna buries her face in my shirt, breathing in my scent, letting the cedar and sandalwood assault her senses the same way I did with her scent. When she steps away from me, I drop my arms, not stopping her. I smile at the way her cheeks are pink, knowing that I did that to her.

Before she can get after me for the kiss, I hold up my hands in surrender. "I know. And I'm not doing anything. I also won't apologize for it."

"I wouldn't ask you to. I wish things were different for us, Will. You, me, and Leo could be so happy if it wasn't for the laws," she says with a wistful tone. I know that she loves him too, but at this moment, I hate Remy for what he took from us. If he'd just been patient, if he hadn't run off, we could all be happy and settled right now. Instead, we're all suffering, and no one can seem to figure out how to fix it. The worst part of it is that he refuses to explain or apologize to any of us. So we still don't really know why he left.

"I know it's not what you want to hear, but maybe you should give him a chance. If you can find a way to forgive him, then we can be together." The words rush out before I realize I'm saying them.

A tear slips down Hanna's cheek. I catch it with my thumb, wiping it away and cupping her face. "I want to, Will, I really do. But he hurt me so badly. And even though he says that he wants to be with me, he still hasn't bothered to apologize or even try to make it up to me."

Her words hurt, but I understand how she feels. "He will, sweet pea. I promise. If I have to beat the idea into him, he will make it up to you. Leo and I will make sure of it. Please just consider letting us court you officially. I hate being so close to you and feeling so far away." The admission costs me, and the look in her eyes is haunted.

But she nods. "Okay."

"Okay, you'll consider it?" I ask, worry seeping away at the idea, but desperate for confirmation.

She shakes her head. "No." Hanna pauses, taking a deep breath.

My jaw drops, and I start to speak, but she holds up a hand and continues.

"I'll accept an official courtship. If you can get Remy to complete the paperwork, and if he'll agree to taking things really slowly, I'll accept. I can't promise that I'll ever forgive him, but it's not fair to you or Leo for me to refuse just because Remy is involved."

She may not realize how much she's still in love with my oldest brother, but I know, and so does Leo. The only other person as clueless as her may be Remy himself. Leo and I are working on them, and this is a huge step in the right direction. "I'll make it happen."

I press a kiss to her cheek, promise to text her later, and dart through the kitchen door before she can change her mind. It only takes Blake a moment to have my coffee and a half dozen cookies ready for me to grab on my way out. I drop a bill on the counter, grab my stuff, and rush away. "Keep the change," I call to him with a smile.

REMY

"She what?" I ask, my jaw dropping at Will's declaration. Normally, I'd be upset that my brother barged into my dinner service at the diner. Especially when Will dragged Leo into it too. This news, however, has taken the bite out of my sour mood.

Will looks from me to Leo and back again. "She agreed to the official courtship. Of course, she has conditions, but that's just a formality. We can work around them. Please tell me that you'll agree and file the paperwork."

I can't find words to respond, so I simply nod my head. We're finally going to get our Omega. I don't know if I'm in shock or in awe of how my baby brother somehow managed to arrange the one thing I couldn't. "What are her conditions?" Leo asks. I'm not sure that I want to know, because I'm certain they have to do with me keeping my distance.

"She wants Remy to agree to moving very slowly and said she's not sure if she'll ever be able to forgive you," Will says. I don't want to agree to that. Why would I?

"No," I say with a shake of my head. I turn back to the stove, plating the entrée I was working on before my brother interrupted.

"Come on, Rem. Don't be that way. You know that she just needs more time. You have to show her that you're sorry," Leo insists.

"Yeah," Will says. "Maybe you could even actually apologize to her."

Shit. I replay our conversation from earlier. He's got me there. I never actually apologized to Hanna for any of this. And I know that I'll have to at some point. Fuck. Why does all of this feel like a power struggle?

four

Placing Bets

REMY

THE KITCHEN IS BUSTLING this afternoon. I'm not sure why it seems like half the town has been in to eat today. I'm not complaining about it, either. Busy days go by faster, but there's no time to even think about anything but preparing orders.

So, when Will drops by to ask if I've filed the paperwork with the Council yet, I growl. "No, I haven't. We're short staffed here, and things have been a little busy the past couple of weeks. I don't see you coming in to cover for me."

Instead of arguing, he rolls his eyes and walks away. What does he want from me? I know I need to file the application. I've had it filled out since the day I got back. It'll get done as soon as I have time. I'm not putting it off. Am I? The Diner has been busy, and we are really short handed. Does that mean that he's wrong for being pissed at me? Not even a little.

If I'm honest with myself, I'll admit that I'm scared. I know that Hanna agreed to accept us, but what if she decides that she can't because of me? What if I'm still not good enough? I can't handle that rejection.

Everyone wants something from me lately, and I don't think I can keep up. My staff wants more help, my brothers want me to fix things with Hanna, Hanna wants...what does Hanna want? An apology? Well, sure, but I don't know how to do that. How do you apologize for trying to make yourself good enough for the love of your life?

Before I can work through any of that, Carrie taps me on the shoulder. "Chef? Remy!" I blink and shake my head, turning to meet her gaze. "I've been calling for you for five minutes. Are you okay?" she asks.

"I'm good. What did you need?" I counter.

"Mr. Sheridan wants to talk to you."

"Was there something wrong with his meal?" I ask, confused about why a customer would want to talk to me unless there was a problem.

She shakes her head. "I don't think so. He ate every bite; even mentioned how good it was. Tipped me double what he usually does. Then he grumbled at me and asked to talk to you."

I'm not sure how to feel about this, but it's not like I can refuse to talk to him. He's a regular and tips the girls pretty well. "Okay. I'll be right out." I take a minute after she walks back into the dining room to clear off my station and wash my hands.

Earl Sheridan is waiting for me at the counter, sitting on one of the bar stools. "Mr. Sheridan, is everything okay? Carrie told me that you wanted to speak with me."

"Boy, I wanna know when you're gonna take your head out your ass," he says with a growl.

"Mr. Sheridan, you are a valued regular customer, but I have to warn you that what you say next will determine if you get banned from The Diner or not," I snarl. Who does this guy think he is, talking to me this way?

"Listen, I'm just trying to help you out. If you don't claim that pretty Omega, someone else will. Hell, my grandsons have been talking about her for a while. So, if you want her, you need to make it clear that she's not available."

"I don't see how that's any of your business. I appreciate the advice, but I'll handle my life my way, thanks," I say, turning back toward the kitchen. I slam through the door, barely missing a collision with Carrie as she runs plates to one of her tables.

The audacity of that old man floors me. And this is part of the reason I left this place. Everyone thinks they can tell you how to live your life or how to handle your business. It's the most ridiculous part of a small town. As for his grandsons being interested in Hanna...I pause for a minute and let that thought sink in.

I mean, Bo, Lucas, and Jesse Sheridan are nice enough guys, but would Hanna really want them? The truth is, I don't know. Can I take that chance?

WILL

I should have known that Remy would flake on the paperwork. I'm not about to get into a screaming match or fist fight with him while he's at The Diner. I have too much respect for our family to do that. Instead, I head back to my shop and brood for a while.

Distracting myself with ongoing projects doesn't help my mood. I find myself almost growling when Lucas Sheridan comes in. "Hey, Will. Is this a bad time? I can come back later," he shouts to be heard over my machinery.

I close my eyes, flipping off the belt sander I was just using. Shaking my head, I drag my goggles off and gesture to the stools near my desk. "It's fine, Lucas. What can I do for ya?"

"Well, I wanted to ask you about something, if that's okay," he starts. "It's none of my business, but I kinda need to know."

"Sure. What's up?" I answer, curious what he could be referring to.

"Are you guys gonna court Hanna Evans?" He holds up a hand before I can form a response. "Because my gramps has made it clear that he'd like for my brothers and I to, uh, entertain the idea. I told him that y'all have all but claimed her, and we weren't getting between that."

"Damn, Lucas. I don't know what to say to that. Yeah, we're interested in her, and Remy is supposed to be taking steps to make it official with the Council. But maybe you should be asking Hanna if she's interested in being courted by y'all." I'd like to say that I'm certain she'll say no, but with all the shit Remy has put her through, she may decide that the Sheridans would be easier to deal with. Fuck, I hope not.

But something like this has to be her decision. "You'd be okay with us talking to her about it?" he asks, confusion marring his features.

I shake my head. "Honestly, no, I wouldn't. But it's really not my decision. If she'd rather be courted by you and your brothers than by me and mine, that's her choice to make. I don't have to like it."

"I don't want to start anything between us," Lucas counters.

"Are you even interested in her?" I ask.

He shrugs. "I don't know; not really, I guess. She's nice and all. We really just want our gramps to leave us alone. And I don't think he's going to if we don't at least talk to her. I was hoping you'd chase me off about it, so I could tell him it's handled."

"Well, in that case," I pause, grinning at my friend. "Stay away from Hanna Evans. She's ours."

He grins back at me. "Thank you. That will get him off my back for a little while, anyway."

"Thanks for coming to me with this instead of just filing the paperwork," I answer. Relief settles over me when he walks out the door, leaving me with the renewed determination to get my brother off his ass.

HANNA

"What the fuck was I thinking when I said I'd accept?" I rant, slamming the cookie sheet in my hand on the counter.

"Woah, there, Han. Don't take it out on the cookies because you're regretting a conversation from two weeks ago. Maybe they changed their minds," Maisy says, grabbing a warm cookie from the sheet. "Mmm, fresh baked oatmeal is my favorite!" she mutters as she takes a bite.

I should kick her out of my kitchen for swiping a cookie and for not being fully supportive of my rant. But she's one of my two best friends, and she'd never lie to me, so I won't. "What do you mean, maybe they've changed their minds?" I ask, a little louder than I should.

"You were questioning your choice, I was offering a possible solution," she counters.

My anger and frustration deflates. "Do you really think they might not want me?" I ask, wiping my damp palms down my apron.

"Only if they've gone completely stupid," she answers. "I mostly just needed you to stop yelling and slamming things around."

"What if that's why I haven't heard anything yet? I thought they were so eager to get this taken care of and make things official. But what if they talked to Remy and he said no?" I know at this point that I'm spiraling, but I can't seem to do anything to make it stop.

"Han, I'm sure that's not it. Do you want me to call Leo to come see you for a minute? I'm sure he can clear this right up," she offers.

I shake my head, fighting against the tears that well up in my eyes. Turning my back on her, I grab another cookie sheet from the oven and set it gently on the cooling rack. When I turn back around, Maisy is putting her phone back in her pocket. I narrow my eyes at her. "What did you do?"

"I sent Leo a text. You need him, Hanna, and of course, he's on his way. Did you know that if it wasn't for Leo, I'd be completely against letting them have you? Yeah, he's that amazing. You already know that, though," she says. Before I can react, Maisy jumps up from the stool she was sitting on, hugs me tightly, grabs two more oatmeal cookies over my shoulder, and runs out the door.

There's nothing I can do now except wait for Leo to get here and see what he says. Mandi pokes her head in a moment later. "Do you want me to bill her for those cookies?" I laugh, because my sister knows I don't charge Maisy or Rissa for anything when they come in here.

"No, but remind me to put her on the schedule for next week while you're at the dentist," I say.

After she leaves, I get busy cleaning up and taking care of finished cookies. I let myself forget about all my worries for a little while, getting lost in clearing the racks and washing the dishes. I'm just finishing up when two strong arms wrap around me from behind.

I nearly jump when his amaretto scent envelops me much the way his arms do. Turning around, I let Leo pull me close and hold me, not bothering to dry my hands. "Maisy said you needed a hug, so I ran right over," he says against my hair.

"Did she tell you why?" I ask, burying my face against his chest, loving the smell of him.

"Not really. Just that you're worried and doubting everything right now," he answers.

I nod. "She's not wrong. About any of it. I did need the hug, and I am doubting everything. Has Remy filed the paperwork yet? I haven't heard anything. Did he change his mind?" I can't stop myself from asking, even though I don't think I want to know.

"I'm so sorry, buttercup. He hasn't done it yet. Debbie went on maternity leave, and he's been preoccupied at the diner," he says. "But he's going to do it. I'll make sure it gets handled first thing tomorrow. Please don't worry."

"So, you haven't changed your minds about me?" I ask, gripping the back of his shirt tightly.

"What? Never. I promise you; we will never change our minds. You're ours. I can't believe you agreed to this, though, since you and Remy still aren't speaking," he says quietly.

"You of all people should know that you can love someone without talking to them," I counter. We've had this conversation several times over the past decade while Remy was gone. Proximity has nothing to do with my feelings for these men, and neither does conversation. It might seem ridiculous, but I know the three of them inside and out.

"Are you going to go through the entire courtship without speaking to him?" Leo asks with a chuckle.

I shake my head. "Probably not. I'm still waiting for him to apologize, though. I'm not ready to give up being mad yet. We both know I won't be able to hold onto it once we're working together for the Founders' Day stuff."

"That's true. You'll forgive him the first day," Leo says with a smirk.

"You wanna bet?" I counter.

"I'm sure Will and I, and probably your siblings, will wager on it," he laughs. I just can't with this guy today. I laugh along with him.

"Well, put me down for a week. I'm gonna try to hold out that long at least," I say, pushing away from Leo. I know what he's done here, and I appreciate it. Using humor to diffuse my fear works wonders.

"I'll do that. And I might just kick my big brother's ass for not filing that paperwork already," he says. I look up at him, my eyes wide at the hunger I see when he looks at me.

"Leo," I say, only to be cut off when he pulls me close and captures my mouth with his. I don't fight the kiss, even though I know that I should. If someone catches us, we'll be in huge trouble. It won't matter that they intend to file the papers. The Council will reject the courtship because we were intimate before things were official. It's happened before, and I'm sure they've been watching us.

LEO

I shouldn't be kissing Hanna right now. I know the laws, but I can't stop myself. I'm a Beta. I should be the level-headed, calm one. Instead, I'm being drug around by my hormones and emotions like a teenage Alpha who hasn't learned control yet. No, that's not it. I'm being led around by my dick. Because let's face it, I want Hanna more than I should.

I kiss her like I'm drowning and she's the last breath of air I'll ever have. Maybe she is. Just when I think I'm about to lose control and take her on the bakery counter, she pulls away.

"We can't. Not yet," she insists.

"I know. I'm—" I start, but her hand covers my mouth, preventing my apology.

"You are not, and I won't let you lie to me," she smirks. "Let's try to forget about this for now. We can revisit after Remy finally takes care of his promises."

She turns from me and goes back to cleaning up the small kitchen. "Are you okay, buttercup?" I ask, wondering if I made things better or worse.

Hanna's smile lights up the room when she faces me again. It doesn't quite reach her eyes, but I can tell that she's not faking it, either. "I will be. I think it's gonna take some time for me to feel comfortable with all of this. Right now, I'm doubting everything. I needed your reassurance."

"Promise me that you'll call or text me next time you start feeling this way. I don't want you to ever doubt your place is with us. And I will do everything I can to force Remy to finish this. I have no idea what's making him put it off, other than stuff at The Diner." It's not a lie, but I know it's not the complete truth, either. If Remy had wanted that paperwork completed, it would have been done two weeks ago.

Once I'm sure Hanna is okay, I head home. This is my only night off from the bar, and I plan to corner my big brother and find out what the fuck he's thinking.

I'm sitting on the couch, watching the door when Remy comes home. "We need to talk," I insist.

"Can it wait? I'm wiped, and really just want a shower and bed," he answers.

I shake my head, standing. "No. This needs to be handled now," I say, walking over to him. "You need to explain why you haven't filed that paperwork with the Council yet. Hanna is gonna back out if you don't take care of it tomorrow."

Remy runs one hand through his already mussed curls, then wipes the other down his face. "Do you want to be the Pack Alpha?" he asks. I can sense that he's about to lose his temper, but I don't understand why.

"No, I want you to do what you promised. For some reason, you're not very good at it, even though you used to be. It would be nice to get off work and come home instead of getting a text that our Omega is having a breakdown and needs her pack, only to realize that she doesn't actually have one because someone didn't do what he promised to," I growl.

Now, I know my brother, and I don't expect this to end well. He's not the type to take me getting in his face in stride. I'm prepared for him to start swinging. What I'm not prepared for is the look on his face when his eyes finally meet mine. Something in it reminds me of Hanna's from a couple of hours ago.

"Leo, I'm trying. I know that I have to file the papers, okay? I'll do it tomorrow morning. You have my word as your Pack Alpha. I don't know why I haven't done it yet," he says, pausing to look at his shoes. "That's not true. I'm sorry. I got scared, and worried that Hanna would change her mind anyway; that she didn't really want *me*, so she would reject us all."

"Rem, I'm trying to tell you that isn't gonna happen. I just spent half an hour reassuring her that the three of us want her. Wait, that's not exactly it. I had to reassure her that *you* want her. Because she hadn't heard anything about the papers and decided that meant you had changed your mind." I pause, waiting until he meets my gaze again. "You two really need to talk about everything. This is getting ridiculous."

Five

One Stolen Kiss

HANNA

WHY DID I EVER agree to go along with this? What was I thinking? I can't be around Remy at all right now. I alternate between wanting to choke him and wanting to choke on him. And his fresh citrus scent is not helping matters at all. My body is practically purring with the desire to lick every inch of this

Alpha. Yet my brain wants to slap that annoying smirk off his perfect face.

"I can't do this," I mutter, looking down at the blank page in front of me. We're supposed to be meeting as team captains to plan out the posters and window decorations to advertise for the Founders' Day Festival. I've barely heard a word Remy has said and haven't taken any notes.

"Look, Hanna, I know that things are tense between us. We should talk about it," he offers, leaning across the table and laying his hand on mine. Fuck. Now I want to lick him again.

Clenching my jaw, I look around The Diner. It's not busy right now, but there are still too many people in here for us to have the conversation that we need to. I shake my head. "I can't do that right now, either."

"I guess I should let Leo or Will be the captain for my team, then. I don't want little miss perfect to be uncomfortable," he snarls. And I'm back to wanting to slap him.

"You of all people should understand the desire to run away when things aren't going the way you expect them to," I retort. It's childish, and I know it will piss him off, but I don't care. If he's gonna be an ass, I'll throw it right back at him.

"You know what? You're right. We shouldn't do this right now. It's only gonna end in a fight. I'll email you a list of my ideas later this week. You can respond or get with one of my brothers. As for the courtship paperwork," he drops his voice lower, "I dropped it off this morning, so you'll have to decide what to do from here about that."

Before I can respond, he gets up and storms into the kitchen. I slip my notebook and pen back into my bag and wave Carrie over. "I'm ready for my check," I say.

She shakes her head. "No can do, sugar. Boss' orders. You don't pay."

I start to argue, but she holds up a hand. "I'm not gonna be the one who goes against what he's said." Carrie walks away before I can respond.

Leave it to Remy to piss me off, get pissed at me, and still be sweet. Fucker. It's so hard to stay mad at him. If it wasn't for how badly he hurt my feelings, I'd probably be throwing myself at him right now. Instead, I find myself walking home alone this cool spring evening.

Relief washes over me when I get home and realize that I have the place to myself. Don't get me wrong, I love my brother and sister. And I completely understand why they didn't want to live at the Patton's when Mom and George got married. I'm sure it's awkward enough for Rissa and her siblings living with our parents.

I lock the door before heading upstairs to my bedroom. All I want right now is a long, hot bath with all the bubbles. I grab my softest sleep pants and cozy sweatshirt, along with my tablet and head to my ensuite bathroom. When the tub is full of steaming water and bubbles, I set the tablet on the counter and turn on an audiobook.

Letting myself get lost in the fantasy story about dragons and their riders, I strip down and slide into the tub. After I scrub at the places where Remy touched my hands and arms today, I sink into the bubbles. I don't fight it when the tears start to fall. How can I love and hate someone so much at the same time?

If I'm being fair, I don't hate him. But I am still pissed at him, and I would really prefer not to love him right now. Since I can't change how I feel, I do my best to calm the tears and consider my options.

I won't refuse the contract. That's not fair to Will or Leo. And it's not fair to me, either. I deserve a pack who will care for me and protect me. I must get lost in my thoughts, because pounding on my bathroom door startles me.

"Hanna! Are you in there?" Henry's voice carries through the small space.

I drag myself from the tub, wrapping my towel around myself and turning my audiobook off. "What are you doing here, Henry?" I ask, making sure I'm covered before I pull the door open.

The sight in front of me causes my breath to catch. And not just because of the smoke filling the bedroom. Henry is in full fire gear, and the house smells funny now that the door is open. "Hanna, I need you to throw on some clothes, fast. The bottom level is on fire, and I need to get you out of here. I'm not trying to get killed for touching someone else's Omega, especially one who's not dressed. Hurry."

He turns his back, and I push the door closed. *The house is on fire!* I throw on my pants and sweatshirt, not bothering to dry off first. I slip my cell phone into the pocket of my hoodie and grab my purse as I exit the bathroom. "Okay, let's go," I say, slipping on a pair of shoes and preparing to follow Henry downstairs.

"The stairs aren't stable; is it okay if I carry you?" The panic in his voice has me nodding in agreement. How did this happen? My head moves as if on a swivel as Henry gently scoops me up and carries me down the stairs. He wasn't wrong about the stairs being a mess. It looks like most of the lower level is destroyed.

What the hell happened here? I don't understand how I went from arguing with Remy to standing outside my house, soaking wet, watching my childhood home crumble.

Arms wrap around me from behind, the scent of dahlia and pear surrounding me. I lace my fingers with Maisy's and accept the comfort my best friend offers. "Leo texted me as soon as they got the call. I got here as soon as I could." I nod at her words, unable to respond.

REMY

I'm sulking in the kitchen after The Diner closes, kicking myself for the way I handled things with Hanna today. I need to apologize and win her over, not push her away. My phone rings, and I almost ignore it. A sense of foreboding makes me take the call.

"Yeah," I answer. "What is it?"

"Hanna's house is on fire. The department just went over. Leo is there, and I'm on my way," Will barks at me, then hangs up before I can respond.

Barely stopping to lock the door, I race out to make sure our Omega is okay. I know I shouldn't consider her ours yet; the paperwork hasn't been reviewed and accepted. But I'll deal with that tomorrow. Hanna needs us right now, and I'm not going to keep screwing this up.

I have to park a block down because of the firetrucks and the crowd. It looks like half the town is out here. By the time I get to her house, there's not much left. Scanning the crowd, I find my brothers before I see Hanna.

"Where is she? Is she okay?" My heart races and I can't catch my breath. I have no idea what I'll do if something has happened to her.

"She's with Maisy; over there," Will gestures. I turn and see Hanna wrapped up in a large blanket with her best friend holding her. It's nearly enough to bring me to tears.

"What the fuck happened?" I ask Leo, focusing on what little is left of the home Hanna shared with her brother and sister. "And what happens now?"

Leo shakes his head. "I don't know. The fire marshal will investigate and determine the cause. We've almost got it out now; at least as much as we can. We'll have a rotation to keep an eye on it in case it flares back up overnight. I'm guessing Hanna will need a place to stay tonight; probably her mom's or Maisy's."

I want to take her home with us. I know we can't, at least not until the paperwork is finalized, but fuck, if only I had submitted it a week ago. Or even three days. But I let my fear hold me back. And now I'll have to suffer being away from my Omega when she needs me. Maybe I can work around this.

"What if we let Hanna, Mandi, and Blake stay with us tonight? At least make the offer. Give them an option, instead of having to go to their mom's where the house is pretty full already," I suggest.

Leo and Will look at me as if I've grown a second head. "That is a great idea," Will says, looking to Leo for confirmation. When he nods, my shoulders relax.

"One of you has to offer, though. She and I had a disagreement earlier, and I don't think she'll agree if I'm the one who asks. I'll happily give up my room for her, though," I admit.

"I'll go with you, but as Pack Alpha, the offer should come from you," Leo insists. The look he gives me leaves no room for argument either. I nod, and the three of us head over to where Maisy is still wrapped around our Omega. If she wasn't also an Omega, I might be annoyed that her scent will likely be all over Hanna now. My brothers follow me to talk to our girl. Hopefully this doesn't blow up in my face.

WILL

I watch Hanna's face as we approach. I want to pull her into my arms and kiss all those emotions away. Unfortunately, we're not alone here, and that would be highly inappropriate. So, instead, I walk over and offer her a soft smile.

Relief washes over her, then when her eyes meet Remy's, she tenses. "Hanna are you okay?" he asks quietly.

"I am. They said I can't go back into the house, though. The first-floor ceiling may collapse, and the stairs are basically gone," she answers. Her expression falls flat, and I wonder if that's shock or annoyance with Remy.

"Where are Blake and Mandi?" I ask, stepping as close as I dare.

"I'm not sure. Neither of them was home when I got here." Her face morphs into panic at the mention of her siblings.

"It's okay, I'll call them," Leo offers, stepping away.

"Just breathe, cupcake," Remy says, rubbing his hand on Hanna's back. I guess we're not going to worry about the laws right now.

"I didn't even know," she sighs, then buries her face in his chest, gripping his shirt. Remy peels his jacket off and wraps it around her, holding Hanna close.

"Come home with us," he whispers, pressing a kiss to the top of her head. "We'll get Mandi and Blake to come too. You guys can stay at our place until you figure out what needs to be done."

"I, I don't know," she says.

"You know the Council won't like that," Maisy says.

"I don't much care what the Council thinks. She's our Omega, and she needs us. Surely, they couldn't argue with that. It's not like we're going to do anything inappropriate," he argues.

"What if we call them and ask first?" I suggest. My brother growls at me, and I back up with my hands raised in surrender. I don't want to fight with him right now. I also don't want to lose our chance with this Omega.

LEO

After I call Blake, I walk back over to Hanna. "Blake is on his way. Mandi is staying at your mom's tonight, but your brother agreed to come to our place. If that's what you want to do," I offer. I won't push her, but I'm sure that Remy has already asked.

Hanna looks up at me, pulling out of Remy's arms. "Yes, please."

The look she gives me has me wrapping my arms around her and kissing her forehead. I know that the smell of my gear won't help her, but she doesn't seem to mind right now. "Go with Remy and Will. I'll send Blake as soon as he gets here, and I'll be home when I can."

As much as I don't want to walk away from her right now, I have to get back to work. My squad has to make sure the fire is out and protect the rest of the neighborhood.

"You'll send Blake when he gets here? And you'll be home soon?" she asks.

"I promise," I answer, squeezing her hand before I head over to check in with my squad.

HANNA

Numbness sets in after Henry carries me out of the house and I stand there watching my past go up in flames. Even Maisy's presence isn't enough to pull me out of the shock I've fallen into.

I'm barely coherent when the Kerrisk boys arrive and offer to take me home with them. I should probably say no, and I'm ready to, until Leo comes back and says Blake will stay there with me. At least this way, the Council won't be able to use this as an excuse to deny their courtship. Understanding that the situation isn't as bad as it seems doesn't make me feel any better about losing the house.

I let Will lead me to Remy's car, climbing into the back seat. He sits next to me and carries me into the house when we get there.

"We'll get you settled upstairs. And we'll take care of anything you need in the morning," Will says. He guides me up the stairs, down the hall to the last door on the left. I should wonder whose room I'm taking, but I don't care about anything right now. I just want to sleep and forget this day ever happened.

As soon as the citrus scent in the room hits me, my eyes go wide. "Remy's room? I can't stay here," I insist.

"Sweet pea, he wants you to. Don't worry, Blake will be next door in the guest room. Remy is gonna crash on the couch downstairs. It's gonna be okay," Will says. "Do you want me to bring you something else to wear? You can take a shower or bath and get changed before you get some sleep."

I nod, not wanting to upset Remy by taking something of his to wear. I'd rather be anywhere but Remy's room right now. The last thing I need is for him to be even more shitty to me because I've taken his room.

Will leaves me alone, and I take in the room that will be mine for the night. There's no way I could stay here more than just one night, especially since our paperwork isn't even processed. The Council would deem it inappropriate, and we'd all get exiled. Having my brother here should be enough to prevent that from happening. I hope.

I smell him before I realize he's standing right behind me. Turning to face the Alpha who broke my heart, I feel tears fill my eyes again. If only I could go back in time and change everything, maybe he wouldn't have left me. I don't have a time machine, though, and nothing makes the pain go away.

Remy and I lock eyes, then he reaches up and cups my cheek. "Are you okay? Were you injured?" I understand that he's not asking about my emotional state, because it's obvious that I'm not okay.

"I'm fine. I didn't even know the house was on fire. Henry saved me," I whisper.

"You could have died," he whispers back, dragging me against him in a fierce hug. It's as if he thinks he can hug me hard enough to put all of our pieces back together. And maybe he can.

"But I didn't," I answer. "I'm pretty sure I lost everything, but I'm still here." The words catch in my throat, and before I realize it, I'm crying again.

Remy holds me closer, pressing kisses to the top of my head. "I can smell the smoke on you. Let's get you cleaned up, okay?" He lets me go only to take my hand and lead me to the attached bathroom. "Do you want a shower or a bath?"

I pause for a moment, considering. I don't have my tablet or my earbuds, so a bath wouldn't be as relaxing as what I'd intended earlier. "A shower is fine. I can handle it."

"You'll need something to wear. Here," he says, opening a drawer and pulling out a soft pair of sweatpants and a tank top. "I'll wash your clothes after you shower. I know this probably isn't where you want to be, but please let us take care of you. We need it as much as you do."

I move to kiss his cheek, but he's faster than I am, and captures my lips with his. My eyes go wide for a moment, then flutter closed as I lose myself in the sensation of Remy kissing me. This kiss isn't languid and sweet. It's filled with passion and desire. Remy wants me, more than I realized. And if I'm honest, it's thrilling to know I have that kind of hold on him.

My fingers fist in his curls. A breathy moan escapes my lips when he tugs me closer, and I can feel exactly what I do to him. I want more, but I know I can't have it. Not yet, not now. Even if the paperwork had already been approved—and I don't know that it has—I can't give in to Remy this quickly. He has to apologize. He needs to understand how badly he hurt me, and he should beg me to forgive him.

A tap on the door has us jumping apart. "What?" Remy growls, his eyes fixed on me as we both pant to catch our breath. The door creaks open, and Will steps inside.

"Everything okay here? I brought Hanna some clothes," he says, holding up a small stack of clothing.

"Thank you. I'm going to take a shower now," I respond, grabbing the clothes from him and dashing into the bathroom. I'm still holding the items Remy handed me. Once the door is locked, I take a deep breath to calm my racing heart. Will's cedar sandalwood scent is on part of what he brought, and I catch a whiff of amaretto, telling me that he brought me something of Leo's too. I lay the clothes on the counter and get the shower ready.

I need this smoke smell gone, and I'm exhausted. I'll deal with everything in the morning. My emotions threaten to overwhelm me, so I push everything away again. Allowing myself to settle back into the numb feeling from earlier will keep me from doing something I'll regret.

REMY

As amazing as that kiss was, I don't expect that to have fixed everything between myself and Hanna. I know she's still upset with me, and she has every right to be. I'm still trying to find a way to apologize. So far, every idea I've had has fallen flat. Nothing is enough.

Once she's in the bathroom, I grab what I need from my dresser and closet. I won't push her for anything while she stays with us. Hopefully, the paperwork will be processed quickly, and we'll convince her to move in with us.

I wish that Will hadn't interrupted us, but it's probably better that he did. Until he starts asking me questions. "So, what did I walk in on?"

With my duffel bag in hand, I shove him out the bedroom door, closing it behind us. "Nothing. Hanna was upset, and I was taking her mind off it."

"Hmm, that's not what it looked like to me. The way you two jumped apart, it looked like you were doing more than talking," he says with a smirk.

"I never said we were talking. I said I was taking her mind off it," I smirk back.

"You know we could get in trouble for that," he argues.

"Which is why I'm out here with you right now," I counter. "It's fine. We're not exactly in public right now. And with what she's been through, no one could blame her for taking a little comfort from her Alpha." I hold up a hand to stop his next argument before he can start. "Yes, I know the courtship hasn't been approved yet. That doesn't change the fact that she's ours."

"Thanks for making her feel a little better," he says before walking away.

Once he's out of the room, I shift my dick to a more comfortable position that hides my erection a little better. Then I start setting up the family room to be my temporary bedroom. It's gonna be a rough few nights knowing our Omega is under the same roof, but we can't touch her yet. Hanna is worth it, though. She's more than we deserve, especially me.

SIX

Was That A Threat?

HANNA

I'M NOT SURE IF I should be pissed that Remy keeps storming into my kitchen, or relieved when he drops the paperwork on the counter with a smirk. I walk over, pick it up, and flip through it without saying a word. The silence that hangs between us is uncomfortable, but maybe that's better than the angry snipping we've been doing. Both have been awkward since I took his room from him since the fire destroyed my home a week ago.

It took him two weeks longer than it should have to deliver the paperwork. Ten years ago, I would have confronted him and asked what the fuck the problem was. Today? I'm just glad he came back. He's been avoiding me for days. Besides, with the official Council seal, this paperwork gives me permission to be intimate with my new pack as we explore and build our connections. And it makes our current living arrangement socially acceptable. Blake will be thrilled to finally be able to find somewhere else to stay.

I can't stop the smile that spreads across my face at the added clause that I'm the one who decides who I spend time with as well as when and how they're allowed to touch me. I know that couldn't have been an easy thing for him to agree to, but he did. Maybe we have a chance after all.

Fighting the urge to run into his arms, I turn to Remy. "Thank you."

"Dinner?" he asks quietly.

I lock eyes with him and raise an eyebrow.

Remy clears his throat. "Would you like to have dinner with us tonight?" That's better. I should say no, because I don't want to make this too easy on him, but I can't.

"You mean, without our live-in chaperone?" I ask, unsure if I want to be alone with the three of them without my brother there.

"I might have already let him know that he can leave whenever he wants," Remy says. At least he has the decency to look embarrassed about it. "Unless you want him there, then I'll call and ask."

I shake my head, trying to hold back a laugh. "It's fine. We can have dinner. Without Blake. But I expect all three of you to be on your best behavior." I hate myself for saying it, because in reality, I want the three of them to bend me over every surface in the kitchen and fuck my brains out.

I have got to stop this train of thought. From the smirk on Remy's face, he can smell my arousal, and that's not helping my case here. "Okay, you have to get out of here. I need to work." I gesture around the kitchen, where I have cookies, cupcakes, and pastries cooling on racks on nearly every surface.

"Fine, I'll go. But don't forget we need to get the posters ready for the window decorating. That's only a couple of days away," he reminds me as he stalks closer. What is he doing?

I can't stop the shiver that runs over me when he stops one step away. "And before I go," he says, dragging me into his arms. "Thank you for giving me another chance." He presses a chaste kiss to my cheek and hugs me tightly before dropping his arms and walking out of my kitchen.

What the fuck was that?

LEO

I almost argued when Remy said he wanted to take the paperwork to Hanna at the bakery. It could have waited until tonight. But he is the Pack Alpha, and technically, he gets to make the decisions here. That doesn't mean I have to like them or even agree. And I'm allowed to voice my opinions. Unfortunately, he has every right to ignore them and do what he wants.

A smile spreads across my face when I get a text from Hanna.

HANNA: *Your brother was just here. I have official paperwork.*

I'm not sure if she's happy about it from the way she worded the text, but before I can ask, she texts again.

HANNA: *And we're having dinner tonight, just the four of us.*

I text back, rushing to clarify what she's saying.

ME: *He didn't demand that you have dinner with us, did he? And are you happy about the paperwork, or upset?*

Instead of texting me back, the phone starts to ring. I answer quickly, desperate to know what she's thinking.

"Now why on Earth would I be anything other than thrilled?" she laughs. I sense her hesitation, but she doesn't sound scared or angry.

"Because our Pack Alpha is a dick?" I offer.

I'm rewarded with another laugh and decide that I'll do whatever I can to hear that sound again, every single day.

"You're not wrong, but at least we get to be a pack now," she counters. "And dinner sounds nice. I told him that the three of you have to behave."

"Ouch," I scoff. "As if my brothers and I would ever be anything less than perfect gentlemen." Hanna's laugh makes me smile, and I'm suddenly excited to have the opportunity to misbehave.

"I have to go now, but would you or Will pick me up after work? I'm sure Remy will be at The Diner until close again, and I don't want to wait that late tonight. I'd like the chance to shower and get ready for my date."

My eyes go wide at her words. *Date.* This is our first real date, and she's excited for it. "Of course. I'll be over after you close to get you. If something comes up at the firehouse, I'll text Will. See you soon, buttercup."

I don't wait for her to respond before I disconnect the call. I need to snap out of this haze before I do something crazy like calling Hanna back and confessing my undying love for her. She's not ready for that, and neither am I. We'll get there soon enough.

Focusing on inventory at the bar is nearly impossible. Finally, I leave Jasper to it and head over to the bakery to wait for Hanna to finish work. If I'm already this far gone less than a day into our official relationship, how much worse will this get?

WILL

I get a text from Leo letting me know that we have a date with our Omega tonight, and I can't stop smiling. My best friend, Sam Nolan, walks into my shop and I turn off the sander.

"What's up, Sam? Haven't seen you in a bit," I say as he walks closer.

"Been busy down at the precinct. Figured I'd let you know that I got pulled to help investigate the fire over at Hanna's," he responds.

"Does it look like arson?" I ask, unable to shake the sudden ache in my stomach.

"Do you know anyone who would want to hurt Hanna, Blake, or Mandi?" he asks, ignoring my question.

"As far as I know, everyone loves them. The only person Hanna has ever had words with is my brother, and I can guarantee he wasn't involved. Does that mean it was arson? Did someone set that fire to hurt them?" My chest aches, and I'm struggling to breathe. If someone tried to hurt them, they may not be safe.

"Right now, we're just looking at all angles. There's no solid evidence of arson," he responds.

"But you have a hunch?" I offer, raising an eyebrow at him.

Sam nods. "I do. I just don't know who would be so reckless. Or why they would want to hurt Hanna or her siblings."

The idea that someone is out to hurt my Omega forces a feral growl from my throat. "If it was arson, you have to find who did this. How are we gonna keep her safe?"

"I heard the papers just went through for y'all. Keeping Hanna at your place should be safer than her living on her own with Blake and Mandi coming and going as they please.

He's staying at our place now, and Mandi is with her mom. If someone is after one of them, keeping them split up is the easiest way to figure out which one they're after," he explains.

I shake my head, trying to understand what he's saying. "Yeah, we just got the papers today. I'm not surprised that everyone knows already. We're supposed to have a date tonight, but maybe it's safer to cancel so we can protect her."

"Nah, man. Have your date. Just keep an eye out for anything suspicious. Give me a call if you need anything or if you see something." He shakes my hand and turns to leave. "And Will?"

"Yeah, Sam?"

"Congrats on finally getting your Omega. I hope y'all are happy together. You deserve it," he says before turning and walking out the door.

With Sam's visit, I know I won't be able to concentrate anymore today. It's not safe to handle the machines if I'm not completely focused, so I shut everything down and clean up. After a quick text to Leo, letting him know I'll be home early, I turn the lights off and lock the shop up.

REMY

Knowing that I'll be going home to our Omega tonight, and that she is finally ours, makes me happy in a way I never thought possible. I want to climb the water tower and scream to the whole town that Hanna is finally mine, and tell the entire town how much I love her.

Since I haven't even given those words to her yet, I think it's better if I don't. Even if it's how I feel, she's not ready for that yet. Ten years of anger and hurt is a lot to let go of, and I haven't even started making it up to her yet.

It's funny how my forced proximity plan barely went into effect when I somehow convinced them all that we needed to make things official. The fact that Hanna hasn't forgiven me is a hurdle, but I'll get past it. I don't care how long it takes for her to decide that she's not mad anymore. I'll wait as long as I have to. She's worth it.

I should explain to her exactly what happened and why I left, but I can't. If I do, it'll just make her more angry. That story paints her father in a horrible light and makes me look like the scared kid I was. I know now that I wasn't ready back then, even if I was too stubborn to admit it then.

Her father's words were only part of why I left. Fear was the rest. I was scared that he was right. I needed to prove to him and myself that I could take care of Hanna the way she deserves. It took me ten long years to get there. Honestly, I'm not sure that I'm there yet. But when Dad passed away, I needed to come home and take over The Diner.

It wasn't fair to leave it to my brothers, who each have their own businesses to run. I had to step up, and that's what I'm doing. How do I convince myself that I deserve her when I can't even figure out how to get her to forgive me?

Maybe my forced proximity plan will come in handy after all. She'll have to spend time with me while we hang signs this weekend and decorate windows. That'll give me a chance to show her I'm not the same kid who left her.

That has to be enough, right? I shake the thought away when Carrie comes in with a complaint about a meal being prepared wrong. Pushing thoughts of Hanna away as much as possible, I refocus on my restaurant. If I don't pay attention, I'll lose everything. And that's not what I want. Destroying the reputation my father worked so hard to build will not help me win over my girl.

"Chef?" Carrie asks, waving a hand in front of my face.

"I'll be right there," I insist, cleaning up my station and washing my hands before following her out to the dining room to talk to the unhappy patron. With any luck, this will be an easy fix, and I'll be back to thinking about my Omega.

I'm not surprised when I see that the patron with a complaint is Sheridan. That old man has it out for me, and I'm not sure why. Except that he told me the last time. He wants Hanna for his grandsons. Well, that's not gonna happen, and the sooner he understands, the better.

Squaring my shoulders, I force a customer service smile onto my face and walk over to the bastard. "Sheridan. Something wrong with your meal?" I ask.

The old man glares at me. "Of course not. I just knew you wouldn't talk to me unless you thought you'd screwed something up again. It's a shame about what happened to the Evans place."

"It is, but everyone made it out safely, and that's what's important," I insist. I'm not sure where he's going with this, but he's starting to creep me out. "What do you want?" I can't stop the question.

"I would love for you to realize that the Omega you're chasing after would be better off with a different pack. When are you going to admit that you're not good enough for her?" he twists his mouth up in something that I'm guessing is meant as a smile. It looks dark and menacing.

"I understand how you feel, and I know there are plenty of people who agree with you about that. But it's not up to you to decide what or who Hanna deserves. Since her father passed, it's her decision. So, unless someone in her family comes to me with a problem, I'll have to ask you to stay out of it." I take a breath to keep myself from jumping the counter and bashing this old man's head on it.

"You'd better watch your back, Kerrisk. Word around town is that the fire wasn't an accident. It'd be a shame if something were to happen to your diner," he sneers, dropping some cash on the counter and storming out.

Was that a threat? Shit, now I'm worried about keeping Hanna safe and protecting The Diner. I walk back into the kitchen, wondering if I should call Sam and report this incident.

HANNA

I can tell that something is bothering Remy when he gets home earlier than expected. "I thought you were closing tonight," Will says.

Remy's growled response echoes as he takes the stairs two at a time and then his bedroom door—the room I've been staying in—slams. Well, fuck.

Will and I exchange a look as Leo walks into the room. "Rem home? What's with the slamming?"

"He's pissed about something," Will offers.

I shrug, unsure if I should go try to talk to him, or let it go. Leo shakes his head and walks back toward the kitchen. "I'll let one of you handle that. I'm gonna finish dinner."

Will looks at me. "You wanna rock, paper, scissors for it?"

I shake my head with a chuckle. "No, I'll go. You get in the kitchen and help Leo. If I need back up, I'll send a text."

The relief on his face is hilarious, but he doesn't stick around for me to enjoy it. Once he's out of sight, I close my eyes for a moment, take a deep breath, then head upstairs. I have an Alpha to calm down.

I stop outside the door for a moment, unsure if I need to knock or if it would be okay to walk in, since he made it clear this was my room until everything gets settled. I decide to call out to him as I open the door. "Remy? Are you okay?"

The room is quiet and dark. I flip the switch by the door and realize that he's in the bathroom. His clothes are discarded by the door, and now that I'm in the room, I can hear the shower running. I understand wanting to get work smells washed away, but there's something else going on here.

His normally fresh citrus scent seems almost burnt the closer I get to the bathroom door. I know that if I walk through that door right now, I'm crossing a line. Remy and I are not ready for this. But I can't shake the feeling that Remy needs me right now. My Omega nature is being drawn to my Alpha, and I'm not strong enough to resist.

I turn the knob slowly, testing to see if it's locked. My eyes go wide when it turns in my hand, and the door slides open with a soft click. A quick glance around the room tells me that Remy has at least contained his temper so far, as there's no evidence of a fist or foot going through the wall or cabinet.

Steam fills the room, and my eyes zero in on movement behind the opaque shower door. I don't want to scare him, but at this point, if he doesn't know I'm here, I have to be prepared for anything.

"Remy?" I say barely louder than a whisper. "Can we talk about whatever it is?" When he doesn't respond, I turn to go. Before I make it three steps, his voice reaches me, filled with pain and anger.

"Don't leave." Those two words are my undoing. The past doesn't matter anymore. I may not be ready to forgive him or forget what he's done, but Remy needs me, and I will take care of him.

seven

Uncomfortable Silence

REMY

I'm nearly blinded by my rage when I get home, only an hour after my confrontation with Sheridan. If it wasn't for Carrie offering to stay and close, I'd still be there, destroying my kitchen and dealing with the aftermath of my explosive temper. I should really give Carrie a raise and a promotion.

That's a tomorrow problem, though. I need to calm down so I don't screw this up with our Omega.

I can't deal with my brothers or Hanna, storming to my room and taking refuge in the shower instead of facing them. I know they'll want answers, and I don't have them. Sheridan is right, I'm not good enough for this pack, and I probably never will be.

But when Hanna risks everything to check on me, I can't let her go. I smell her before I realize she's standing halfway between the door and the shower. She says something I can't understand with the noise of the shower, then turns to leave. I know it costs her to come to me like this.

I'm barely able to rasp the two words that keep her in here with me. "Don't leave." I should let her walk away. A better man would revoke the courtship offer and send her out to find a pack that can protect and care for her. But I'm not a better man. This Omega is mine and I need her right now, laws be damned.

I lift my head, locking eyes with her. What I see there nearly destroys me. I expect pity, but all I see is concern and something that might be deeper than I'm ready to discuss. Without a word, eyes still on mine, Hanna starts stripping out of her clothes. I barely hold back my groan when she's standing in front of me, bare.

We can't do this. We can't do this. I repeat to myself, even though I know it's pointless. I'm so far gone that if Hanna can't pull me back, I'll lose everything.

The moment she opens the shower door and steps inside, my breath hitches. When she wraps her arms around me, I hug her to me tightly, burying my face in the soft skin between her shoulder and neck. As much as I want to be strong, there's something about this tenderness, from the one person who has every right to hate me, that breaks me.

Anger ebbs as the tears start. I should push her away. I absolutely should not kiss her again. But even as I have the thought, I find myself lifting my head and turning toward her. Hanna lifts a hand to cup my cheek, and I press my lips to hers.

I know without words that she's accepting me, all of me, even the parts that she can't stand. Even as I wish I was a better man, I'm relieved that I'm not. Our kiss is slow at first, heat building between us with every moment we're connected.

HANNA

I have no idea what I'm doing. I mean, obviously I'm kissing Remy, but on a larger scale. How did we go from snipping at each other earlier to making out in his shower? I have no idea, but I'm determined to find out. First, I'll give my Alpha what he needs, then I'll worry about answers.

My hand that cups his cheek moves into his hair, tugging him closer. I know that this is going to end with us fighting again, but I can't find it in me to care right now. There was no choice in this—he's mine, and he needs me.

"Remy," I breathe against his lips.

"Cupcake, I need you," he rasps. I nod, kissing him again. When he doesn't move, I gently take his hands that are wrapped around my back. I slide one down to cup my ass, and bring the other up to cover my breast.

"I'm yours," I say, pressing a kiss to his throat. "Take what you need, Alpha."

A heartbeat later, I find myself pressed against the shower wall with Remy ravishing my mouth. Whatever had him frozen has worn off, because his hands are everywhere, igniting fire along my skin with each touch. We work each other up nearly into a frenzy, touching and kissing, stroking and licking.

When he releases me and steps away, fear races through me. Has he decided that he doesn't want me? I don't think I'll survive another rejection like that. Before I can fully spiral, he drops to his knees, easing my leg over his shoulder and running his nose along my mound, breathing in my scent.

As if I wasn't already dripping with slick, I feel another gush at the sensation. Remy hums his approval, then rakes his tongue from my opening to my clit. I gasp as he slides his tongue inside me a few times before moving his attention back to my sensitive nub. When he starts to suck, and slides a finger into my soaked pussy, I come undone. My hands fist in his hair, and I grind against his face, riding out my climax.

"Such a good Omega, giving your Alpha your orgasm like that," he praises, looking up at me from his knees. "So wet for me. Just for me right now, yeah?"

"Just for you, Remy," I breathe as he laps up my release. I don't know how much more I can take before I'm begging him to knot me. And I don't think we're ready for that emotionally. Not yet. I close my eyes and take a couple of deep breaths, then pull him to his feet. "My turn," I whisper, kissing him hard before I drop to my knees in front of him, turning his back toward the wall.

"Hanna, you don't have to," he starts, but I cut him off by dragging my tongue along the tip of his cock, licking up the bead of precum and stealing his voice. Before he can protest, I suck him into my mouth, curling my tongue around him. Relaxing my throat, I take him as deep as possible, loving the way he tenses and gasps at the shock of it.

After taking him deep, I back off his dick, licking the length of it as I watch his face. When I take it deep again, his eyes close and his head falls back against the wall. "Fuck, Hanna. You're killing me," he breathes. I notice that the burnt edge to his scent is gone, replaced with a heady freshness that tells me exactly how much he's enjoying this.

High on this power I have over my Alpha, I focus on bringing him pleasure. I put everything I have into this, determined to make him lose control. It's what he needs, and I know it. I bob on him, fucking my mouth with his cock, pausing to tease the tip before doing it all over again.

After a few times alternating with my mouth and hand, I'm swallowing as fast as I can to catch his release. Once I've licked him clean, he pulls me to my feet.

Without a word, he kisses me long and slow. When he pulls away, he turns and grabs the shampoo, washing then conditioning my hair for me before washing my body.

I rinse off and try to return the favor, but he shakes his head. Remy pulls me close and presses a kiss to my forehead. "Thank you." He takes a deep breath, then whispers, "But if you touch me again right now, I will knot you, and I don't think we're there yet."

"Oh," I answer, my eyes wide. Because he's right, and I can't argue about it. We're not ready for that. I nod, backing slowly to the door and stepping out as quickly as possible. After wrapping myself in a towel, I scoop up my clothes and dress quickly in the bedroom while he finishes his shower.

For a moment, I worry about what Leo and Will are going to think when we both come downstairs freshly showered. Then I realize that our courtship was approved, so I haven't done anything wrong. Besides taking care of Remy first, that is.

WILL

"What is taking them so long? She went up there to talk to him, and it's been more than an hour," I rant at my older brother. Patience is a virtue, but it is one I do not possess.

"I'm sure it's nothing to worry about. She's just calming him down so we can enjoy our dinner together. They'll be down as soon as they're ready," Leo says, opening the oven door to check on our food.

He levels me with a glare, as if he can read my mind. It's not that I'm jealous of my oldest brother getting Hanna's attention. It's that he hasn't earned it. As far as we know, he still hasn't apologized or explained why he left us all. That's what pisses me off.

I decide to change the subject because I really don't want to fight with Leo. He may be a Beta, but he's almost twice my size and I'm not sure I'd win.

"Lucas came by the other day. His gramps is pushing them to try for Hanna. He all but begged me to warn him off," I laugh.

"At least he understands the situation. His grandfather is a dick," Leo says.

"More than you know," Remy responds from the doorway. We turn to see him standing there with an arm around Hanna's waist. Maybe they've made up, then. It doesn't matter if I think he got off easy; forgiveness is her decision.

"What do you mean?" Hanna asks, looking up at him. He guides her to the table, pulling out a chair for her to sit. Then he looks at us.

"Dinner ready? Or do we have a few minutes?" he asks.

"We have a few minutes. What's up?" Leo answers.

"Let's sit, and I'll explain." Fuck, that doesn't sound good. Leo and I take seats at the table, turning our full attention to Remy as he begins his story.

My oldest brother explains how the old man suggested a few weeks ago that we either needed to claim Hanna or make it clear we didn't want her. Then how he came in suggesting that if we didn't let his grandsons have her, it could get bad.

"Wait, he didn't really make it sound like he'd had something to do with the fire, did he?" Leo asks, eyes wide and fists clenched.

Remy nods. "He did. And he suggested that it could happen to The Diner, too. I don't think the old man could have set the fire, but he could have convinced one of his grandsons to do it. You know those boys worship him."

"I'd guarantee it wasn't Lucas, and that he didn't know anything about it. I was telling Leo earlier that he came to see me. Asked me to warn him off pursuing Hanna so he could get his gramps off his back about it. There's no way he was involved in this," I insist.

Remy and Leo nod. "If I suspected any of them, it would be Bo. He seems the most likely," Leo says.

"Agreed. But Jesse can't be discounted, either. He's always been a little obsessed with our girl. Could have been both of them working together," Remy responds.

Hanna's eyes go wide. "What? Jesse Sheridan is obsessed with me? How did I not know that?"

I laugh. "Because you're a sweet person who sees the best in everyone." The glare I get in response is enough to make my brothers laugh along with me. "I didn't mean it in a bad way."

"She doesn't see the best in everyone, just most people," Remy counters. I know he's talking about himself. A pained look crosses Hanna's features, and I know he's not wrong. I hope they can figure out how to fix their relationship soon. It's becoming clear that whatever happened upstairs helped, but wasn't enough.

LEO

The oven timer goes off and I check our dinner. This lasagna is taking forever. Or that's how it feels. Today has been the longest day in existence, and I'm ready for it to be done. I can tell that the double shifts I've been putting in are pushing me toward burnout.

"We should let Sam know about our suspicions," Will says when I walk back in carrying the lasagna and garlic toast.

"Is he the one investigating? Have the officially ruled it arson?" Hanna asks as I walk back into the kitchen for the salad. Remy follows me, grabbing drinks for everyone.

"He stopped by and said it's leaning that way. That's why he's already looking into it. I'm sorry, Hanna," he says quietly.

"There's nothing we can do about it now. I just hope that the insurance covers the damage," she answers.

"Once they're done with the investigation, it'll be easier to sell the place," Remy says. I glare at him as I serve our dinner.

Hanna's jaw drops. "What?"

"When the investigation is done and the insurance is settled, we'll get it sold. John said that even without the house, the property is pretty valuable. It's not like you need it now," he answers.

How does he not see that he's pushing her away right now? This fight is the last thing the two of them need. We're supposed to be courting her, not chasing her out of our lives.

"Rem, maybe we should talk about this later," I suggest.

"What's there to talk about? Hanna doesn't need the house anymore—she lives here now. Blake has somewhere else to stay, and Mandi has moved in with her mom. It only makes sense to sell it and split the money between the siblings," Remy says, as if it's not the most horrifying idea he's ever had.

I watch Hanna's expression, waiting for her to blow up at him. Her jaw clenches, and I can see that she's trying to hold back the explosion. He doesn't deserve this girl.

"Let's not ruin our first dinner as a pack with an argument," Will insists. "Just table it, Rem, and enjoy dinner. There's plenty of time to discuss and decide what to do."

"There's nothing to discuss. It's pointless to hold onto the property. We have this house, our home. Hanna is our Omega, so she lives here with us now. Her brother and sister are settled and don't need the property, so there's no reason not to sell. Yeah, we have to wait until the insurance is settled and the investigation is over. But that's it," he argues.

I wait for Hanna to lose her temper, barely holding mine back. We exchange a glance and she shakes her head slightly. I decide that I'll follow her lead and stop arguing with my idiot brother. He can't see that he's hurting her with this. Or he can, and doesn't care.

The rest of dinner is weighed down by uncomfortable silence from our Omega. Hanna refuses to speak, and I can't say I blame her. Eventually, Remy gives up on trying to start a conversation and we embrace the discomfort. When we're finished eating, Will offers to clean up and Hanna disappears upstairs. I expect to hear Remy's door slam again, but it doesn't.

I climb the stairs slowly, intent on making sure Hanna is okay. Remy's door stands open, and it's clear that Hanna has removed everything of hers from it. Interesting. I can't help noticing that my door is closed now, and I usually leave it open. Even more interesting.

I tap on the closed door, giving her a minute to decide if she'll let me in. "Can I come in, buttercup?"

She pulls the door open and stares at me. "It's your room, Leo. Of course you can come in." I can't help wondering if that means she's planning on staying in here with me, or if I'll be taking the couch tonight. The couch is probably a better idea. She needs some space and privacy after what Remy just pulled at dinner.

"I just need to grab a few things, then I'll get out of your way," I offer. The moment I cross the threshold; she wraps her arms around me and breaks into tears.

"Please don't leave me alone tonight," she whispers. I pull her closer, holding tightly in an effort to stop her tears.

"Whatever you need," I offer.

"Let me stay in here with you," she answers. I don't think that could be any more clear, so I nod. If she needs me to lean on, I'm here. That doesn't mean anything sexual will happen. I mean, we've been an official pack for less than one full day, and our Alpha is already screwing everything up. Part of me wants to head back downstairs and beat my oldest brother's ass until he understands what he's done wrong.

That won't help our Omega to feel better, so I put that idea away. "For as long as you want. And if you want me to give you some privacy, I will. I want you to consider this your room now, and I'll just be here when you want me to." I have no problem letting her have the room. I'd sleep on the floor outside her door if I had to.

I just want her to understand that she is my top priority. "I'm sorry," she says. "I don't want to put any of you out of your rooms. I just can't stay in his room right now, and I don't want the guest room. I don't think I can even talk to him."

"You have nothing to apologize for, buttercup. He's being a dick, and he knows it. Please don't worry about it. I'll take care of it," I promise, still holding her tightly.

EIGHT

Half Frozen

HANNA

"He did not," Maisy insists, swirling her coffee cup before taking a swig.

"I bet he did," Rissa argues. "He's such a dick."

I shake my head at my besties, appreciating how they don't jump to Remy's defense over the big announcement from last night. "He most certainly did. And I didn't know how to react.

Leo and Will tried to convince him that we needed to talk about it, but his mind is made up."

"Did you at least rip him a new one?" Rissa asks, taking a bite of her pastry.

"Nope, I didn't say anything. For the rest of dinner and haven't said a word to him since. I'm sure he knew I was pissed. Still am." My cheeks warm as I say the words. I have nothing to be embarrassed about, but I feel like my friends will judge me over this.

"Honestly, Ris, the silent treatment might be more effective. I think he likes it when they fight," Maisy says with a smirk. "Hate sex is hot."

"And how would you know?" I counter. I don't have a problem talking to my girls about my sex life, but until yesterday, none of us were supposed to be doing that.

"I know things," she laughs. "Unless the Council asks, then I have no idea what you're talking about."

The three of us collapse in a fit of laughter. This is what I needed today. Time with my besties and an outlet for my rage so I don't take it out on anyone but Remy.

"Is it wrong that I want to find a way to get back at him? It's not like he's wrong about the situation, but the idea that I have no say is infuriating," I say when our laughter fades.

"Oh, please tell me we can help you plan it," Rissa insists, rubbing her hands together. She really is an evil genius, and I should let her help me. But I shake my head.

"It's better if I handle it myself. I don't want to drag any of you into this," I answer.

"What about the fire? Do you think Sheridan or his grandsons could really be behind it?" Maisy asks, effectively distracting Rissa from her torture plans for my Alpha.

"It looks that way. As far as I know, there's no evidence. But the guys were gonna call Sam and talk to him about it," I answer. "The whole thing has me scared. What if it happens again, and someone gets hurt. Or worse."

A shudder tears through me, and I close my eyes against the idea that someone could get hurt because of the pack I chose to be with. Omegas are more rare than Betas, but it's not like there are so few of us that people need to fight like this.

After a pause, I look at my girls. "Can we talk about something besides me for a while? I need to take my mind off things."

"We could talk about how cozy Rissa has been while hanging out with my brothers," Maisy offers. Rissa shoves her in mock anger.

"Or we could talk about you spending so much time with the Nolan boys," she counters. Their interaction makes me laugh. They go back and forth, each trying to outdo the other with scandalous stories about bending the rules just enough to stay safe, but still having bonding time with their potential suitors.

"I kinda hope that your situation pushes Joey to ask Dad about courting me. Every time I bring it up, he changes the subject," Maisy says with a sigh.

"I've been waiting for your brothers to finally see me that way for a long time," Rissa admits. "It seems like they might actually realize that I'm a grown woman now."

And now we can see the hazards of growing up in a small town as an Omega. We spend so much time together as families that us girls may have developed crushes on our guys before they were ready to consider us. Maisy's brother Aaron is a little older, and always treated all of us like his little sisters. It's driven Rissa crazy for years.

"How would my situation push any of them? You think the fire will motivate them to finally push for a claim?" I ask, not understanding what she means.

Maisy shakes her head. "No, Han. Not the fire. The courtship papers—since Remy finally manned up and filed them, maybe that's what will push Joey to get moving. I'm not getting any younger here."

We crack up again, because Maisy is always making jokes about being old. She's only a couple of years older than me. "You are not old, grandma," I tease.

And just like that, my worries are forgotten for a little while as we talk about everything.

WILL

I should be at my shop right now, working on the new kitchen table for Mrs. Patton. Instead, I'm helping decorate windows for the Founder's Day Festival. How did I get roped into this again? Oh, yeah. Remy. My brother decided that it would be easier to get Hanna on board for our teams working together if Leo and I were on his team.

With a sigh, I grab another poster and tape it to the window. One look at the stack has me growling. Mandi looks at me with wide eyes. "Sorry, I'm annoyed at Remy, not you," I say with a smile.

"I understand. This isn't how I wanted to spend my morning, either," she answers as she tapes a different poster to another spot on the window.

"Yeah, we got the crap jobs this time," I agree.

A grin spreads across her face and she giggles. "We should protest and make Remy do the next activity by himself!" I understand her hesitance to have my brother spending time with her sister, even with the courtship in place. I have the same reservations. But Hanna promised me this morning that she would be okay, and I have to take her at her word.

LEO

"That's the last one," Blake says, wiping his hands together in an 'all done' gesture. A smile spreads across my face, because I know this means I can go pick Hanna up from Maisy Watson's house where they've been having a girls' day.

After Will and Mandi left with their stack of posters, Hanna told me she wasn't feeling up to spending time with Remy. Of course, I called Maisy and arranged for them to have some time together. And my brother may not fully agree with my declaration that he deal with his posters on his own, but since our Omega refused to go with him, there wasn't much he could do.

"Fantastic! That means I can pick your sister up for lunch," I say.

"Why is she so mad at Remy this time? If you don't mind me asking." Blake cocks an eyebrow at me with the question.

"He told her at dinner that he's gonna arrange to sell the property after the investigation and insurance is dealt with," I answer.

Blake's eyes go wide. "What? He didn't bother to talk to her about it before making that kind of decision?" He pauses, taking a deep breath. "You know, if I wasn't one-hundred-percent certain that my sister loved him, I'd beat his ass."

"I still might," I counter. Blake and I laugh.

"You know what? I think I'm gonna text him and see if he wants some help with his posters, since he's on his own," he says with a mischievous grin.

"Give him hell," I answer, heading out the door.

"Oh, I will," he answers. His laughter follows me as I head toward my truck. I have a date to pick up, and an Omega to pamper.

REMY

I know this is a punishment, and even though I'm the Pack Alpha, I'll take it. I upset my Omega, and I'll pay for that. Then I'll make her admit that I'm right. Should I have talked to her about it before making the declaration about selling her parent's property? Probably, but that doesn't mean that I'm wrong.

To be fair, I'm a little pissed that they all wanted to argue about a sound decision made by their Alpha. I'm already making major concessions for Hanna to make this courtship work. The fact that one conversation last night caused her to move out of my bedroom and shack up with my Beta brother is proof that we're not completely ready to forget the past.

I didn't expect to win her over instantly, but after what happened in the shower—nope, stop thinking about that. There is no way I'm going to put up all these posters on my own while sporting wood because of an encounter with my Omega.

Well, that thought didn't help. My phone pings, and for a second, I think maybe it's her. Perhaps she's feeling guilty about ditching me today and wants to help me with the rest. Instead of a text from my girl, I find one from her brother.

BLAKE: *Where are you? I'll take pity on you and help you finish your list.*

Blake offering to help should be a good thing, but I can't help wondering about his ulterior motives. Did Hanna put him up to it? Is he coming to start a fight with me because I pissed off his sister? I guess we'll find out, because I'm way too desperate to get this done to turn down the possibility of help. I text him with my location, and that I'll wait for him.

A few minutes later, Blake walks in and I don't think he's pissed. "Hey, Remy. You didn't do too bad on your own," he says, looking at the posters I have left.

"Would have been easier if your sister hadn't bailed on me," I admit, shaking my head. As much as I don't want to get into this with him, maybe he can help me convince her that my idea isn't horrible.

"I heard all about it from Leo. That's kinda why I offered to help you. I have a proposal for you, and it might get you out of the doghouse with Hanna," he offers.

"We can talk while we work. Next one goes across the street," I gesture at the next building on my list and we start walking.

"I'd like to buy the lot and rebuild the house. I was planning to talk to Hanna and Mandi about it once things were settled, but..." he trails off.

"But I opened my big mouth and fucked it all up?" I offer with a smirk.

"Exactly," he says. "So, what do you think? I know as her Alpha, the title technically goes to you, but I'd like to make sure she's okay with it, too."

"I think that's probably the best option for everyone. It should be enough to appease her and my brothers. As far as I'm concerned, it's a deal," I respond, offering my hand to shake.

"I'm still gonna talk to her about it, because the last thing I want is to be on her shit list. No offense," he smirks.

"I have a feeling I'm gonna be there for a while," I counter. "And it's not like I really deserve not to be, either. I've been fucking things up with Hanna for a long time."

Blake smiles at me. "Don't give up on her. Keep doing what you need to in order to make things up to her, but don't give up. She'll come around. I know she's mad, but more than that, she's hurt. Maybe consider giving her an apology and an explanation?"

I nod my agreement, and we get to work hanging posters. Relief washes over me when he changes the subject. A couple of hours later, we hang the last of the posters and head home. I expect a cold reception when I walk in, since Hanna wouldn't speak to me last night.

HANNA

Spending the day with my girls was exactly what I needed to figure out how to handle my anger and resentment toward Remy. It's not fair to any of us for this tension to be hanging over us.

After Leo picks me up, we have lunch and do a little shopping for my nest. I know it won't be long before my heat hits, and I'm not very excited about it. I used to dream about my first heat with my pack. We'd connect, make love, and they would claim me. That was all I ever wanted. But with the disconnect between Remy and me, I don't know how it's going to go.

We have to talk about it together, which means no more silent treatment for Remy. I'm not sure I can handle that, but I'll have to. I can't keep freezing him out when he says or does something to offend me. Otherwise, I'll never speak to him again. Because if there's one thing Remy Kerrisk is good at, besides being ridiculously hot, it's pissing me off.

Leo, Will, and I are watching a movie when Remy finally gets home. I fight back the pang of guilt I feel at leaving him to put up all the posters on his own. "Don't go easy on him. He deserves worse than you gave him over it," Will says, somehow knowing what I'm thinking.

"I know, but it still wasn't right of me," I counter. I won't fight with them tonight. We have to talk about everything and act like adults. But I can't change their behavior; all I can do is focus on mine.

"Hey," Remy says when he walks into the living room. Another pang of guilt hits me at the sad expression on his face when he sees me sandwiched on the couch with his brothers. It almost makes me want to jump up and move to another spot. Almost.

"Hey," I answer, barely glancing toward him. I don't want to give him power over me right now. I'm sure he's pissed that I ditched him, even though he deserved it.

"We should talk. All of us," he says, sitting in a chair across from the couch we're on. I tense at his words. This doesn't sound good. My heart races as we all turn to face him.

Will turns the movie off, and we wait for Remy to speak.

"I understand that I upset you, Hanna, by deciding to sell what was your family home without discussing it first. You have to understand that I didn't do it to upset you. It's the only logical decision," he starts.

"Except that it's *my* decision," I argue.

"As the Pack Alpha, I have every right to make that decision for you. And I won't apologize for doing my best for this pack," he says.

Rage burns behind my eyes as I stare at him. What made me think agreeing to courtship was a good idea? I have no proof that Remy is capable of change. And I'm not some weak Omega who will bow down and do what she's told, no matter how badly I want a pack to take care of me. That kind of relationship has to be built on trust. If I'm being honest, I don't know if I can trust Remy.

That thought hurts, but there's nothing I can do about it. If he doesn't respect me enough to allow me to be part of the decision when it's my childhood home being discussed, then I don't know if I can be his Omega.

"I know you're pissed, and that's fine. You'll get over it. I found a buyer for the property today, and I wanted to let you know that I'll be moving forward with a deal. If you want to freeze me out, go ahead. I'm the Alpha, not you. I will not argue or debate every decision I make. This is not open to discussion," he insists.

Leo and Will glare at him, fists balled in their laps. I look at each of them before standing and walking toward the door.

"No one is arguing over your 'power,' Remy. You're not being challenged. But this is not what I agreed to when I signed those papers. There are clauses to prevent this exact situation from happening. I'm sorry, I can't do this." I turn and walk out the front door without even stopping for my shoes. I'm not taking anything with me, especially since these guys have insisted on buying everything I have now because of what I lost in the fire.

I'm better off on my own. I have my phone in my pocket, and it's not too cold tonight. I walk down the street toward the bakery. Shit, I should have grabbed my purse so I would have my keys. Oh, well. I can text Mandi or Blake and get them to come unlock it for me.

I make it three blocks before Leo's truck pulls up beside me. "Hanna," he calls as he pulls over. "Please get in the truck. I grabbed your purse and shoes. You shouldn't be walking barefoot, much less alone after dark." Something in his expression makes me waver in my intent to leave, and I find myself climbing into the truck.

"I can't go back there," I say quietly as I pull on my shoes and fasten my seatbelt. When I turn to face him, Leo is staring at me with tears in his eyes.

"I wondered how long it would be before Remy completely fucked everything up for us. I guess I have my answer now. I'll take you wherever you need to go. Whatever you need, Will and I are gonna support you," he says.

Fuck, this is the worst. How can I turn my back on these men I love? No, I have to. If Remy can't understand what he did wrong, then there's no hope for us. Especially when he never bothered to apologize or explain why he left. I need to be with a pack who will respect and care for me, and that's not a pack that includes Remy Kerrisk.

"I'm sorry, Leo. I never meant for any of this to happen. It was stupid of me to think that he might have changed. Unfortunately, I think we were doomed before we ever got a chance. I wish I could change things, but I can't be with someone who doesn't respect me. Will you please just take me to the bakery?" I ask, hoping that he can somehow understand how I'm feeling.

He nods and pulls away from the curb, heading toward my business. Even with the heat on in the truck, I'm shivering by the time we arrive. "Here, buttercup, take this. You're half frozen from walking barefoot. I won't ask you to give him another chance. He doesn't deserve it. But would it be okay if I text you tomorrow? I need to know that you're okay," he says, pulling his hoodie over his head and handing it to me after he parks in front of the bakery.

I take the hoodie, pulling it over my head and sniffing deeply. I know that part of why he's giving it to me is so I have his scent. "Thank you, Leo." I lean over and press my lips to his, since technically we're still able to be affectionate until I cancel the contract.

Our kiss is tender and sad. Leo's lips ghost against mine, so gently, it's as if he's scared he might break me. And maybe he is. But it's too late for that. His brother broke me a decade ago, and is still ripping out pieces of my heart now. As hard as it is to say goodbye, I grab my purse and climb out of the truck.

I don't look back when I open the door and step inside, but I hear Leo's truck pull away after I've closed and locked the door. I should call Maisy or Rissa, but I can't right now. I should text Blake or Mandi, but what would I even say?

I walked away from the only pack I've ever loved because the Alpha is a disrespectful asshole. That's what I would say. And that's not what I want my family to think, so I'll keep it to myself. When I tell them about this tomorrow, I'll claim that I can't get over Remy leaving. This will be my fault, and I'll be the bad guy.

It's better than he deserves, but I can't drag him through the mud. It's not fair to Will or Leo. The truth would damage their reputation as much as their brother's. And no matter how angry I am at Remy, his brothers don't deserve to suffer because of him.

I double check the front door and the back door. When I'm satisfied that both are secure, I lock myself in my office and curl up on the small couch. It's not comfortable, but it'll do for tonight. I plug my phone in, noticing that I have texts from all three brothers.

Unable to deal with my emotions, I turn the phone face down on the table and try to sleep. When I can't hold them back anymore, tears fall, soaking Leo's hoodie and diluting his scent. At some point, I must fall asleep, because I wake to the noises of early morning prep.

NINE

Don't You Dare

HANNA

THE NEXT TWO WEEKS are a blur. My family and friends ensure that I'm never alone, even if I want to be. At one point, I start lying about staying with Maisy to my family, telling Maisy I'm at my mom's, just so I can have some peace and quiet. Sleeping in my office isn't ideal, but it is quiet. I ignore texts and calls from Remy, refusing to speak to him at all.

I text with Will and Leo, but only until one of them says something about the pack. Then I disappear for a while. I even call the mayor's office and drop my team from the competition. I can't afford to do it, but with the way things are, I don't have a choice. I can't be around the Kerrisk boys right now.

It's gotten to the point that when one of them comes in the bakery, I lock myself in the office until I know they're gone. If Leo or Will stand in front of me and ask me to come back, I know I just might do it. I can't let myself, though. I hate Remington Kerrisk with everything I have. Just as much as I love him.

The Founder's Day festival brings in some new faces and business picks up a bit. It's nice to stay busy. The day before the baking competition, I wake up in my office after another restless night. I don't feel well, and debate calling Rissa to take me to Mom's. I decide that it's not worth exchanging comfort for interrogation. Instead, I curl up on the sofa again, tugging Leo's hoodie over my head and sinking into it.

He and Will have taken to dropping off a freshly scented one a couple times a week, even if I won't talk to them or see them. He left this one for me yesterday, when he picked up the one Will had left a few days ago. Snuggled up in it, with his scent surrounding me, I let myself doze off while my brother and sister take care of the bakery. As much as I want to get up and go help them, I just can't.

Everything hurts, I'm hot and cold at the same time, and sweat trails down my spine. When the cramps hit, I know exactly what's happening. I am fucked. My heat is starting, and I have no one to turn to. It's too late to schedule with the

Omega Care Center. They wouldn't take me anyway because I have a pack now.

And as badly as I don't want anything to do with Remy, as an Omega, I know I need him for this. I don't have to want him, though. I fight against the urge to call for as long as I can, then dial Leo's number.

"Buttercup, is everything okay?" he asks, as if he can read my mind.

I try to answer, but pain takes over and I sob into the phone. "Hurts. Need you," I pant, barely audible over the sounds of me crying.

Panic is evident in his voice. "Were you in an accident? Where are you?"

"No accident. Heat starting. At bakery. Please, Leo," I beg, fighting the tears back as another wave of nausea hits.

"Fuck. I'm on my way," he says. "We'll take care of you." His promise echoes in my ears as he disconnects the call.

LEO

The moment I hang up the call with Hanna, I dial Will. "Hanna is going into heat. I'm picking her up now. Get Remy and meet me at home. We're gonna have to set up a nest, get food and drinks together, and take care of her all at the same time."

I don't give him a chance to argue, disconnecting and dialing Maisy as I speed down the street toward the bakery. "What the fuck do you want?" she starts when she answers.

"That's a hell of a how do you do, now then isn't it?" I retort.

"Sorry, I thought you were Remy. He's called me six times today, and won't take no for an answer," she responds.

"Hanna's going into heat. Can you get some snacks and drinks together and drop them off at my place? I'm on my way to pick her up now," I tell her.

"I'm on it. Do you need someone to cover the bar for a couple of days?" she offers.

"That would be great. Can you take care of it?" I ask. "Jasper should be able to help, too."

"We've got it handled. Take care of our girl. And make your idiot brother behave himself, or I'll deal with him," she threatens.

"I'll do my best, but you know Remy as well as I do." I disconnect the call as I pull up to the bakery. I leave the truck running and dash inside.

"Hey, Leo. You know she doesn't want to see you right now," Mandi starts when she sees me.

I shake my head. "She called me; I'm here to pick her up." I motion for her to come to the edge of the counter, a look of apology for the customer she's helping. "Sorry, but your sister is going into heat. Can you take care of the bakery for a few days? I'm taking her home with me, and I promise we'll make sure she's as pampered as possible."

Mandi's eyes go wide and she nods, pulling something from her pocket and pressing it into my hand. "She's locked in the office. I need those back when you go, so I can get in and lock up at night."

"Thank you," I say, taking the keys and rushing down the small hallway. It takes a moment to unlock the door, and when I do, my heart breaks for what I see.

Hanna is curled up on the couch with my hoodie wrapped around her. She has her face buried in it, using my scent to calm her down. "It's okay, buttercup, I'm here. Let's get you to your nest, okay?" I speak softly, knowing that she's not thrilled about this situation. I don't want to upset her any more than necessary. We should discuss the contract and claiming, but I can't bring that up when she looks this miserable. "I've got you, baby," I whisper, scooping her up and carrying her through the dining room.

I don't bother to say anything to her sister, nodding my thanks to her and the guy who holds the door for us. I toss her the keys on my way out the door. I get Hanna buckled into the truck and rush home. My heart races the whole way.

WILL

Leo's call catches me off guard. We haven't even discussed Hanna's heat, especially since she left us. I can't blame her.

I'm barely speaking to my oldest brother, and now I have to convince him to come with me. Like that's gonna happen.

Most likely, he'll glare at me or take a swing. It won't matter to him that Hanna needs all of us right now. The Diner will probably be his focus, and what's best for the pack will be ignored again. What else can I expect from Remy? It's what he's done as long as I can remember.

I have to try, anyway. I rush into the diner, heading toward the kitchen. I know it's not an ideal time, but this can't wait.

"What the fuck are you doing in my kitchen?" Remy growls when he looks up. I stand in front of him, panting.

"I need you to come with me. Get someone to cover the place for a few days," I insist.

"Fuck off," he says, turning his back on me.

"Hanna is going into heat. Leo is taking her home—to our place. I guess if you get your head out of your ass, you can help us take care of our Omega. If not, I probably wouldn't bother coming home," I snarl, storming out the door.

In my truck, I take a moment to calm down. Driving in this condition is not a good idea for anyone. Before I can put the truck in gear, Remy jerks the passenger door open and hops in.

"Let's go. Hanna needs us," he says simply, pulling the seat belt around himself. Well, fuck me. My brother actually does care about someone other than himself. Wonders will never cease.

With one final look behind me, I back the truck out and tear down the road toward home, and the Omega I hope will let us claim her.

REMY

When Will shows up in my kitchen, interrupting service, I'm pissed. He hasn't talked to me since Hanna left us. What the fuck could he want now? But the moment he says she's going into heat, everything changes.

I take two seconds to ask Carrie to handle things, explaining as much as I can about why I'm disappearing. She's dependable and capable of running the place without me. I barely make it to the truck before Will leaves. Or so I thought. When he sees me, he freezes, as if he didn't think I was coming.

Damn, I have really fucked things up; not only with Hanna, but with my brothers, too. If they don't even trust me to be there for our Omega when she goes into heat, there's not much hope for us as a pack. I can't help wondering how she'll react to the nest we've been putting together for her. Will she even want me there? Or will I be forced to stay outside, delivering water and snacks? It would serve me right if that's all she wanted me for.

I've been a total ass, even if that wasn't my intention. All I ever wanted was to provide for my family; for them to be proud of what I'd accomplished. Instead, I'm on the verge of losing everything. I can't stand by and let that happen. I have no idea how I'm going to fix this, but I will.

Maybe it's time to stop trying to do everything myself. That realization hits me like a truck, slamming into my chest. Should I tell them all the truth about what really happened all those years ago? I don't know that I can. Hanna doesn't deserve to know how awful her father was to me.

The more I think about it, the more I wonder if I'm viewing that memory accurately. I've spent years replaying his words in my head, colored by my disappointment at being refused. So much time spent convincing myself that I had to prove him wrong. But was any of it necessary?

In the end, I think all I did was prove to myself that he was right. I wasn't ready back then. Am I now? I want to be.

Will parks the truck and rushes inside. "I'll be right there," I call after him, stopping to gather up the supplies someone left on the porch. Probably Maisy, since Rissa is at the bookstore today. I hope she had help getting all this together. Making a mental note to repay this kindness, I carry everything inside, making three trips to get it all.

I toss some of the drinks into the fridge, checking the bags to make sure everything else that needs to stay cold goes in there too. As I work, I consider what I can do to finally prove to Hanna that I'm not going anywhere. The truth is a start, but it won't be enough. Even understanding that everything was my fault, my youth, my ego—doesn't fix it.

Vowing to give Hanna what she deserves, I grab a few of the snacks—a bowl of mixed fruit, a bag of mixed nuts, and a variety of chocolate bars, and a few drinks, then head upstairs to the nest. I know that's where my brothers are with our Omega, and putting this off won't do anything to help me.

HANNA

By the time Leo gets to me, I'm a mess. I barely remember the ride home, then he carries me up the stairs to a room I've never seen. A nest! Did they do this for me? Guilt washes over me for running away. Even if Remy deserves my anger, Leo and Will don't.

While I'm still coherent enough to express myself, before the Alphas get here, I decide that I need Leo to understand what I want. "Leo," I start.

He cups my face with one hand, easing me down on the mattress inlaid into the floor. "You don't have to say anything, buttercup. We'll take care of you. I'll make sure no one claims you. We can talk about the details later. Don't worry about it right now. It's okay," he insists.

The love shining in his eyes destroys me. This man will fight off his brothers to make sure they don't do anything that takes advantage of me.

I shake my head. "No, Leo, I want you to claim me. All of you. I'm still mad at Remy, and he owes me apologies and explanations. But I love all of you, and want to be yours," I say.

His eyes go wide. "Does that mean you'll stay?"

I close my eyes against the tears that threaten to overflow, nodding. I can't leave them again. I'll rage against my Alpha as much as I need to, but I won't leave again. That nearly killed me.

"Forever?" His whispered words force the tears from my eyes.

"Forever," I agree.

"I will beat Remy's ass for almost ruining this," he growls.

"Don't," I argue. "I'll handle him."

Leo leans down and captures my lips with his, the kiss tender and gentle. Which means it's the opposite of what I want right now, as another wave of pain courses through me. I cry out against his mouth, and he pulls me closer.

"Leo, it hurts," I pant, wrapping my arms around him in a desperate attempt to pull him closer than he already is.

"I know, buttercup, but Will and Remy will be here soon. Let me help you," he says, easing away from me and laying me back against the pillows. "Just lay back. I'll distract you until they get here."

The pillows surrounding me are velvety soft, and I burrow into them a little when he releases me. That doesn't last long before he's pulling me up to strip off my clothes. In my pain-filled haze, I'd nearly forgotten that I'll have to be naked for them to care for me during my heat.

I whine at the chill from the ceiling fan blowing on my heated skin. Leo's eyes meet mine, and he drags his shirt over his head with one hand, dropping it onto my chest. It's warm and carries his amaretto scent on it. I sigh, bringing it up to my nose and inhaling deeply.

When his tongue laps at my entrance, slick gushes, and I gasp. "It's okay, buttercup, I'll take care of you until our Alphas get here." I hum at his words against my soaked pussy. Leo goes back to worshipping me with his tongue, stroking it lazily along my slit. The contact helps with the pain, but doesn't make it go away.

Leo slides two fingers through my slick, thrusting them into me as his tongue strokes against my clit, lighting up that little bundle of nerves. He crooks his fingers, hitting the perfect spot to make me come undone. I cry out with my orgasm, my back arching off the pillows, before flopping back down. The pain subsides a little more, and I feel more like myself.

I know it won't be long until the pain returns, and with it the lust-filled desperation to be knotted. And as much as I love Leo, he's not going to be able to help me with that. Before I can express those concerns, the door opens and Will rushes in. Well, one Alpha is better than none, I suppose.

"He wouldn't come?" Leo asks. Will ignores him, dropping down next to me and kissing me. It looks like it may just be the three of us, then. I tell myself that it's okay. I can't make Remy want me, any more than I can make him understand how badly he upset me with his "I'm the Head Alpha" bullshit. This is okay. I knew this was a possibility when I accepted the courtship contract. At least he included the clauses that put me in control here. Otherwise, I could lose everything.

I get lost in the feeling of Will's lips against mine, so gentle, almost teasing. I tug at his shirt, but he's not patient enough to take it off. Instead, he reaches between us and a moment later, I feel his cock notched at my entrance.

Slick gushes from me again. "Yes, please. Knot me. Claim me. Will, I need you." I don't even care that I'm begging; I'm that desperate. Our eyes meet as he slides inside of me in one thrust.

"Oh, Hanna. You're so slick for us. Feels so good," he moans. I meet him thrust for thrust, lifting my hips as I chase the friction that feels so good. I lose myself to the passion between us as Will guides me toward my next orgasm.

I'm not sure where Leo disappears to, but I'm too distracted to worry much about it. Will pounds into me over and over, feeling better than anything ever has. Closing my eyes, I let the pleasure wash over me as his knot swells, locking us together. When I finally open my eyes, they land on Remy, standing in the doorway, staring at me.

He looks half-starved, as if I'm his next meal. Part of me is completely and totally here for it. The rest of me hesitates because he's still just standing in the doorway. What is he waiting for? Why isn't he in here with me? Doubt creeps in again, and I shake my head to clear it.

No, this isn't happening. If he doesn't want me, then he has to tell me. "Remy," I breathe, staring at him.

He turns to leave and I cry out, "Stop."

Will freezes against me, as if holding still would deflate his knot and stop him from finishing his orgasm. I pull him down to me for a kiss, and he seems to understand that I didn't mean him.

When I look up again, Leo is shoving Remy into the room. "Our Omega wants you in here, too, dumbass," my sweet Beta tells his brother.

"Hanna, I'm not—I don't have to—fuck. Give me a second," Remy says, closing his eyes and taking a couple of deep breaths. "You don't have to include me. I won't force that bond on you. If you want my brothers, and not me, I'll accept that."

He might be willing to accept that, but I'm not. "No."

Remy stares at me even after I answer with that one single word. "Okay, I can go."

"Don't you dare," I respond. "Get over here and help your Omega through her heat, you idiot." His eyes go wide, as if he can't believe what I've said. Leo shoves him again, and he closes the distance between us.

Momentarily sated, I relax against the pillows as Will's knot finally goes down and he slides out of me. I can't help feeling like Remy may have ruined Will's experience with knotting me, but Will isn't the one who looks upset.

"We'll give you two a minute," Will offers, moving to stand.

I shake my head. "No, we're not doing this. Not now. I need all three of you, and none of you are going to make excuses and leave me. Not until this heat is over."

Will and Remy blush, clearly taken aback at being scolded by their Omega. Leo laughs. "I told you both it would be this way," he says, bringing me a soft blanket and cleaning me up with a warm rag. "And she's right, we should talk before she needs us again."

He steps away again, and I watch, ready to get after him too. But he drops the rag into a bin near the bathroom, then turns to the fridge I hadn't noticed before. "Maisy got snacks for us. Everything is handled at the bakery and the bar," Leo says, bringing a bottle of water and bowl of mixed fruit over before dropping down beside me.

I gesture for Remy and Will to sit, surprised when they actually do as I've asked. Leo hands me the bottle of water and sets the bowl of fruit in front of me.

"Does our courtship contract give me the power to decide who knots me and when, as well as who claims me and when?" I ask, glaring at Remy. I know the answer, I just want to see if he'll admit it.

"It does. That's why I was going to leave," he says.

I shake my head again. "You're not leaving. None of you. If we're doing this, then we're all doing this. Yes, my heat is coming. Fast. But I'm still able to make decisions right now, and I want this to be clear." I level each of them with a stare, making sure they're paying attention.

"You two," I point at Will and Remy, "are going to knot me throughout my heat. And all three of you are going to claim me. Tonight. Understood?" It's the most demanding I've ever been with them, and I'm not sure if Remy will go along with it or fight back, since he craves control.

"Anything you want," Leo says from my side.

"Agreed," Will answers.

I focus on Remy, willing him to respond.

TEN

Completely Satisfied

REMY

Hanna stares at me. After her declaration, I'm not sure what to say. I want to believe that this is her choice, but I can't understand what would make her include me.

"I, I don't know," I stammer.

"Look, we're gonna fight. It's kind of what we do now. That doesn't change the way I feel about you. I've always cared about you, even when you ran off without bothering to say goodbye. Ask your brothers; they'll tell you. It's the reason I've never dated anyone else or entertained other courtship offers." Hanna's words floor me.

I figured she'd had offers. She's gorgeous, and a genuinely beautiful person inside and out. There had to be other offers. But she never considered any of them? I look at Leo, then Will. Without even asking, I know she's telling the truth. How many offers were there? How much did she sacrifice while I was gone?

Guilt eats at me, even worse than it did before. "You could have, though," I admit. "It would have served me right."

"Would you stop being so stupid? I didn't want anyone else. I still don't. You three are mine, and I'm yours. So, unless you really don't want me, we're gonna have to figure all of this out," she says.

"How could I not want you? I'd have to be dead, and even then, I would want you more than anything. I know it's not an excuse, but everything I've done has been for you. I know that's not enough of an explanation," I admit.

"But we don't have time to get into all of it right now. So that much will have to do for now," Leo says, pulling Hanna into his arms as she breaks out in a sweat and her eyes go glassy. "The fever is taking over again. Are we good?"

I meet my brother's gaze and nod. "Good enough until Hanna's heat is over. Then we all need to discuss this more." I won't hold back from knotting or claiming my Omega, now that I know it's exactly what she wants, even if she's pissed at me.

Hanna cries out in pain, and my brothers look at me. It takes me a moment to realize that they're waiting for me to reach out for her. Leo and I strip down, and I wrap my arms around Hanna, pulling her to my chest.

"It's okay, cupcake, we'll take care of you," I whisper, peppering feather light kisses on her cheeks. She groans, and I bring my lips to hers. Hanna wraps her arms around my neck, holding on as if letting go would mean saying goodbye forever. I can feel her desperation already, and we're not even bonded y et.

Her lips are soft and sweet, just like they were a decade ago. Kissing her feels like coming home, and I wish I never had to stop. I know that won't get her through this heat, though, so I pull myself back when I start to get lost in our kiss.

HANNA

The moment Remy's lips touch mine, I feel like everything is going to be okay. I'm still desperate for his knot, but I know it's coming. He'll never deny me again after tonight. Once we're bonded, he won't be able to. None of them will. Of course, neither Leo nor Will has ever wanted to deny me anything.

My skin feels like it's on fire, then Remy's hands are there, heating me up even more. He strokes a hand down my back, teasing his fingers along my spine. His other hand cups my breast, pinching my nipple before sliding down my stomach toward my core.

"Remy, please," I breathe when his lips leave mine to trail down my neck.

Instead of answering me, he trails his hand lower, barely stroking against my clit before rubbing his fingers through my slick-coated folds. I jerk my hips, trying to push him to touch me the way I want. I know he's not going to let me lead, though, when he pulls his hand away, wrapping the other around my waist to hold me still.

As soon as I stop moving, he goes back to dragging his fingers through my wetness. I whimper, looking over at Will when I can't get Remy to do what I want. "Please, Will," I beg. He looks at his older brother, then back at me. For a moment, I think he's going to give in. Then he shakes his head.

"Trust me, cupcake, I've got you," Remy whispers against my ear. I whimper again, wishing it was a growl instead. I hate feeling so desperate that I'm willing to beg. "Give up control and let me take care of you, Omega." His words are hot against my ear, spoken softly enough for me to be the only one to hear h im.

I nod, willing my body to relax against him. It takes a minute, but then he hums his approval when I finally manage to untense my muscles. "Good girl," he purrs in my ear.

Remy seems empowered by my submission. He strokes a finger against my clit, rubbing circles around the sensitive nub. "Oh, yes, right there," I encourage. He gives me a look, and

I bite my lip. Apparently, I'm not supposed to let him know what I like, either.

He must know what I'm thinking, because he smirks at me. "I can tell what you like and what you don't by your body's reaction. Now stop trying to boss me around. I'm in charge right now. Got it?"

I whimper again, but nod. I don't want to give up control, especially of my pleasure. But I know that if I try to fight him on this, he'll stop touching me and I won't get his knot. I can't let that happen. I need it. I need him.

Once he's sure I'm following directions again, Remy thrusts two fingers into my slick heat, curling them against the spot that melts me. I cry out, wondering if he'll get after me for that, too. When he doesn't, I suppose letting him lead isn't so bad. He works me up until I'm shaking and on the verge of an orgasm. But he doesn't let me fall over that edge yet.

"Not yet, cupcake. I want you to come on my cock," he says.

"Yes, please," I breathe. "I want it. So bad."

Remy's eyes blow wide with lust, and I know I'm about to get what I want. He flips me onto my back and spreads my legs wide, staring at my exposed body. Just when I think he's going to thrust into me, he pushes back and drops his face between my legs.

His tongue laps at me, swiping through my slick coated opening before swirling around my clit. "Mmm, so delicious," he growls against my sex. "Such a pretty pussy. It's gonna look amazing taking my knot."

His dirty talk riles me up more, and I start to buck my hips against his face. Remy pauses again, giving me a look that freezes me in place. His hands stroke up my body, cupping my breasts again before he removes them.

The lack of body heat against me makes me shiver. Before I can fully process the loss, Remy's body is over mine, and he's sliding inside of me. He sets a slow, torturous pace, as if he has nothing better to do for the rest of his life but slide his dick into me and pull it back out.

"See? What did I tell you? So beautiful, taking me like this," he mutters as he strokes slowly into me again.

I groan at the blissful, almost painful sensation. "Remy, please. I need more."

The desperation in my voice must set him off, because suddenly, he can't thrust into me fast or hard enough. My cries of pleasure fill the room, along with our scents. Within moments, the room is fragrant enough that Leo has to turn the fan up.

He and Will are just watching as Remy fucks into me over and over. Each thrust pushes me closer to my next orgasm. I need it so badly I can't stand it. Just when I'm about to start begging again, Remy reaches between us and pinches my clit, sending me over the edge.

While I'm coming, his knot swells, and I can feel his release shooting into me. He bites down on my neck, right above my scent gland, claiming me. My breath catches and I gasp at the sensation as his teeth sink into me, breaking my skin and sealing our fate. We're permanently connected now.

Taking Remy's knot is the most delicious feeling, and I can't wait to do it again, even though we're not done yet. As I come down from my latest orgasm, Remy brushes my sweat soaked hair from my brow.

"Bring her some water," he barks at his brothers. "And more of that fruit. She needs to keep her strength up."

As annoyed as I usually am when Remy goes full Alpha, this time, it's hot. Probably because it's centered around caring for me. I don't know how long we can make this peace last, but I'm determined to enjoy it while it does.

With his claim, our bond snaps into place. I can feel his emotions, not exactly as if they were mine, but enough that I know he's nervous about this. Even if he's being dominating and acting confident, I know better. Somehow, it's comforting to know I'm not the only one who's a little scared of this decision.

Leo hands Remy a bottle of water while Will feeds me some of the watermelon from the fruit mix. Remy takes a drink, then offers the bottle to me. While I drink deeply, he holds perfectly still, careful not to set off another wave of pleasure that could choke me. It's thoughtful that he's being so careful with me. The idea gives me hope for our future.

I'd been a little annoyed that Will hadn't claimed me earlier, but now I understand why he waited. It would have been awkward for all of us if Remy had refused if the other two had gone through with it. A yawn tears out of me as my body relaxes, finally sated. "It's okay, cupcake, just rest. We'll clean you up and tuck you in," Remy whispers against my ear as I drift off. I pass out with his knot still inside me.

LEO

Once Hanna falls asleep, I encourage my brothers to do the same. "You won't get much rest once she wakes up. This is just the start of her heat; it's only going to get more intense," I explain.

When Remy is able to pull away from her, he takes the rag I offer and cleans her up before taking care of himself. "You'll need rest too," he insists, bringing a bottle of water with him when he comes back from the bathroom.

"I'll have more chances than you will," I say, knowing that Hanna won't be as desperate for my attention as she will for my brothers' since I'm not an Alpha. "And I'll wake you both when she needs you."

Will settles in on one side of Hanna, and Remy lays down on the other. I wait a few minutes after they fall asleep to make sure Hanna stays asleep. Now that everyone else is taken care of, I can restock the mini fridge and snack cabinet.

Twenty minutes later, I drop down to the inset mattress where the rest of my pack is sleeping. Hanna looks adorable sandwiched between my brothers with a pile of soft blankets on top of her. I pull a blanket over myself, content to watch them sleep until I finally doze off.

HANNA

I wake to pressure holding me still. For a moment, my heart races and I fight against it. Then I realize that I'm in my nest, and the pressure is actually Will's arm and Remy's leg, both of which are thrown over me as they sleep on opposite sides of me.

I take a couple of deep breaths, remembering why I'm here and what happened before I fell asleep. I press my hand to Remy's cheek, dropping a kiss on his forehead. This bond has to help us fix our relationship. If it doesn't, I'm not sure I'll survive.

Pulling my hand away from him, a wave of pain hits. I want to let my Alphas rest as much as I can, but I don't know how to relieve this pain without waking them up. I manage to wiggle out from under their limbs, sitting up against the fluffy pillows. From my new vantage point, I can see that Leo fell asleep at my feet.

In some ways, he's meant the most to me over the past decade. Because of Pack Law, and him being a Beta, we've grown closer than I am with Remy or Will. Leo's Beta nature allowed us more alone time to talk than I had with Will.

I love them all, and hope that Will understands what I'm about to do. Because I've waited long enough for my sweet Beta to claim me. It's not typical for a Beta to claim an Omega, but I'm insisting this time. No, he can't knot me like his brothers, but I will wear his mark the same as theirs. And no one will talk me out of it.

Carefully, I climb over the pillows surrounding me and the two Alphas still sleeping. I notice that Leo is the only one wearing clothes, even if it's just a pair of shorts. Not for long, though. I toss a blanket over Will, then another over Remy. These guys are horrible about kicking covers off in their sleep.

Then I turn my attention to Leo, carefully peeling his shorts off, before dragging the blanket off his chest and replacing it with my feverish skin. "Hanna?" he whispers when he realizes what's happening. "Are you okay?"

"I will be as soon as you fuck me and claim me. I need you, Leo. I want your mark, too," I say, leaning close to his ear. He shivers as my breath tickles his skin.

"You do? I thought," he starts, but I cut him off by capturing his lips with mine. The kiss is hard, all passion and need.

"Stop thinking. It's overrated. Just fuck me instead, then when you make me come, claim me. Please, Leo, I need you," I beg, not caring how desperate I sound. I will get what I want; I just have to convince him that he wants it too. "Unless you don't want me," I pout. Yeah, that'll do it.

The look on his face changes and he flips me onto my back. "Oh, buttercup, I want you more than you realize. I just didn't expect you to want my mark the same as your Alphas. I figured you'd be more desperate for their knots than my ordinary cock."

I stroke a hand between us, gripping said cock tightly and stroking it. "I would hardly call this ordinary, Leo."

He growls as I stroke him while rubbing his tip along my slick coated core. When he finally gives in and pushes into me,

I groan in pleasure. "How do you want it, Hanna?" Leo purrs in my ear, and I melt at the way my name sounds on his lips.

"Fast and hard, Leo. I need to come," I answer, tilting my hips toward him as he thrusts into me again.

While he's thrusting into me over and over, pounding harder and going deeper, he trails lazy kisses along the skin of my neck and down to my collarbone. Leo traces his brother's claim mark on my neck with his tongue and I shiver at the sensation it causes.

I groan when he stops moving and stares down at me. Then I start to feel self-conscious. "What's wrong?" I ask, locking eyes with him as a goofy grin spreads across his face.

"You're so beautiful. I want to remember this forever," he says, leaning down and kissing me gently as he starts to move again, gliding into me and pulling out again.

Frustrated, I huff at him. "Leo, please."

"I mean it. But I understand. You want to come, and you want to be claimed. So, come for me, buttercup," he says, sliding a hand between us and pinching my nipple.

I cry out with my release, gripping him tightly as he thrusts into me again and again. When he finally follows me over the edge, his release shooting inside me, Leo leans over and bites my shoulder. His teeth break my skin, and I come again. I wasn't expecting to have the same feeling of completion when he claimed me that I had with Remy, because Leo is a Beta, but I do. I can feel him in my head. It's a strange sensation, but I like it.

WILL

I'd thought watching Hanna with my brothers would be weird, at least at first. Somehow, it's the most natural thing I've ever done. I know she belongs to each of us, the same way we all belong to her. When she comes with Leo, my cock throbs with the need to take her.

I'll admit to being a little jealous that Remy got to claim her first, but Leo and I had discussed it before. Now that both of my brothers have claimed our Omega, it's my turn. I know that even after an intense orgasm like the one she just had, she'll still be desperate for a knot.

Handing my brother a warm rag, I pull our girl from his arms. "My turn," I say to him. "You ready for this knot, sweet pea?" I ask Hanna. Her eyes go wide and she nods.

I kiss her, hard and deep, then flip her around to sit on my hard length with her back pressed against mine. From this position, I can easily lift Hanna and thrust into her from below. After a couple of minutes, I realize that I won't be able to keep up this pace as long as I'd like to.

Shifting her to her knees, I push her gently down on her elbows to support herself. Reaching around her waist, I trail my hand down to stroke my fingers along her clit as I pound into her. I know that our Omega likes it hard and fast, and I plan to give her everything she wants.

My knot swells inside Hanna when she comes, gripping my cock like a vice. I feel my release spraying inside her, and bite down on her neck, between my brother's marks. Our bond snaps into place, and I know that I've completely satisfied her for now.

Hanna sighs, relaxing as I ease us down on our sides to wait for my knot to release. She doesn't fight against sleep as it takes her under, trusting us to clean her up and let her rest. When she wakes again, we'll have to get her to eat something. For now, I wrap my arms around her and watch as she sleeps.

ELEVEN

A Complete Loss

HANNA

WHEN I WAKE UP clear-headed on what I think is the third day after we entered my nest, I stifle a happy squeal. Days of knotting, fucking, and gloriously delicious dirty talk from my Alphas and Beta fill my mind as I remember the lucid moments of my heat. Make no mistake, these men are mine. Nothing will tear us apart now. Even as I think the words, I can't help remembering that I'm supposed to be mad at Remy.

We'll figure it out, I remind myself. *Every pack has issues. We just have to communicate. Which Remy is not good at. Ugh, we're screwed.*

I don't let the negativity take hold, pushing it away to focus on the feeling of my three new bonds. I'm not sure how common this feeling is. Pack bonds are not something we learned about in school, and most people keep their pack business private from those outside of their pack.

Mama never wants to answer questions, so I'll have to adjust to this on my own. I can see the appeal of keeping it a secret, though. Having one thing that only exists for the four of us is thrilling. It makes me feel even more connected to them.

After spending a crazy amount of time watching my men sleep, I decide to shower and get some real food. I wonder if there's anything to eat in the house, since my heat came on suddenly, and we didn't have warning to prepare.

I use Leo's shower, put on my own clothes for the first time in days, and enjoy a few minutes of peace and quiet searching the kitchen for something to make. I find a hastily scrawled note on the counter.

Stocked the fridge for you. Figured you'd be too exhausted to cook with all the noise coming from up there. Call us! ~ M & R

Of course, my best friends would find a way into the house while we're locked away in the nest. And it doesn't even surprise me that they took care of meals for us. I open the fridge and gasp. They weren't kidding. There are at least three days' worth of meals in here. A quick perusal of options has me grabbing a breakfast casserole.

I turn on the oven and put the dish inside to heat slowly. I make a pot of coffee, taking a cup to the living room and settling on the couch with a book while I wait for breakfast to be done.

"Something smells good, and I'm not talking about my Omega," Leo says as he enters the room. He gestures to my cup when he leans down for a kiss and I nod toward the kitchen. Without another word, he goes to get his own.

Will slides onto the couch on my left, taking my cup out of my hand and drinking deep. "Oh, yeah. Perfection." I swat him, then pretend to ignore him for my book. He laughs, then continues drinking my coffee. Jerk.

A plate appears in front of my face, steaming breakfast casserole making my stomach growl. I look up to see Remy standing there. "I brought you food, and another cup of coffee," he offers.

"Thank you," I say, taking the plate from him and digging in. I expect him to set the cup down and walk away, but he drops onto the couch on my right, holding it. "You don't have to do that," I suggest, but he shakes his head.

"I'm taking care of my Omega," he insists. The thought is sweet, sending tingles straight to my heart. "How are you feeling today?"

I pause between bites to answer. "I probably won't be running a marathon today, but I feel good," I tease.

"When we woke up without you, I thought maybe you'd run off to the bakery," Leo says, dropping into a chair on the other side of Will, who is still making a show of enjoying my coffee.

"As much as I miss it, I don't think I'm up to that today. I'll have to get back to it tomorrow, though." I know that most likely, Mandi has been running things, and I'm sure she could use a break. "It's been three days, right?"

"Um," Will says, his eyes wide. He looks from Remy to Leo.

"What? Heats usually last about three days," I say.

Remy takes the plate from my hands and sets it on the coffee table, along with my mug. Then he takes my hands in his and tugs until I lock eyes with him. "From what we were taught, yeah, three days is normal. But yours was a bit longer."

"How much longer?" I ask. I'm not thrilled at the idea of losing time.

"Leo brought you home a week ago," Will says.

"Seven days?! There's no way," I insist. How could my heat have lasted for a whole week?! I've never known of another Omega who had a heat that long. Does that mean there's something wrong with me?

Leo looks at me. "It's true. I slipped out and texted Maisy when it was apparent that this wasn't a normal heat. That's why we have food. And why our businesses are all taken care of."

I try to jump up from the couch, but Remy pulls me onto his lap, banding his arms around me. "I have to go. Mandi is gonna be pissed that I've abandoned her for so long," I cry, tears filling my eyes.

Remy presses a kiss to my temple. "No, cupcake, she's not. I talked to her this morning, while I was making your plate. She's fine. Yes, we're gonna owe her a vacation, but she understands. This isn't like you just took off for a week. You are an Omega, and your heats are a natural part of your cycle."

"What about Leo's Place and The Diner? And Will's shop?" I ask, panic setting in at how much my heat could have ruined things for my guys.

Will reaches over and threads his fingers through mine. Leo laughs. "It's all handled. Will's clients have been contacted. They're fine with waiting a little longer for their custom orders. The bar and the diner have been running the same as if we were there."

"But how?" I ask, still not understanding what he's saying.

"Jasper is taking care of the bar, and Simon has things handled at the diner," Remy answers. "They're both capable, and have a decent support system that consists of our friends to help them out. Same with the bakery. Everyone pitches in when an Omega goes into heat, especially when it's the first one with their pack."

Oh, shit. That means that everyone knows that they've claimed me. I expect to be embarrassed about that, but the familiar warmth never comes. "Okay, that's a good point. And I know that we'll have to do the same in the future. It's just hard to let go of my responsibilities, ya know?"

The look all three men level on me is heated and reproachful. And then another realization hits. "Wait. You said it's been a week?" I stare at Remy with wide eyes.

"Yeah. It's been seven days since any of us have left this house," he answers.

"So, you missed the Founder's Day baking contest?" Guilt washes over me at the thought of causing him to lose the competition because he had to be here with me. My eyes go wide and my jaw drops.

Remy nods. "I did. But so did you."

Shaking my head, I argue, "No, I withdrew after our fight."

"I know, and I talked Mayor Berry into adding you back in. I was planning to goad you into competing against me," he says with a smirk. And while I should be annoyed that he went behind my back, I'm touched that he understands how important that contest was to me.

"Well, it's too late now," Leo shrugs. "The contest is over, and there won't be another chance until next year."

"I think it all worked out, though," Will adds.

In one way, I agree. But knowing that I lost my chance at the prize money makes me sad. I'm not sure what I'll do if I have to close down the bakery. For a moment, I forget that they can sense my emotions.

"Why are you so bummed about it? I thought you'd decided you didn't want to compete," Remy says, trying to get me to look at him.

"You're an idiot, Rem. She needs the prize money to keep the bakery going. That's the only reason she was going to compete in the first place. How did you not know that?" Leo growls.

I feel Remy's eyes on me, and I stare at the floor as my cheeks heat. He reaches up and tilts my face, forcing my eyes to meet his. "Is he serious? The bakery is at risk? I had no idea things were that bad," he says.

"We were barely making it when you came back to town," I admit.

"Fuck," he swears. "So, I really was putting you out of business with my breakfast stunt. Damn, I'm sorry, Hanna. I thought they were exaggerating because I'd upset you. I fully expected you to show up at The Diner and chew me out. That's the only reason I made those changes."

Tears fall as I realize that the whole reason I'm going to lose my father's dream is because Remy wanted to force me into a confrontation that I was too scared to give him.

REMY

Leo's claim that Hanna's bakery is about to go out of business seems ridiculous until she confirms it. Shame washes over me. How could I be so selfish? Trying to goad her into a confrontation could have ruined her livelihood. What kind of man does that to the woman he loves?

"I'll fix it," I insist when her tears start to fall. She shakes her head, covering her face with her hands.

"You can't," she argues.

"I'll find a way," I say. There has to be a way to encourage people to go to the bakery without taking business away from The Diner. No matter what it takes, I'll figure it out. I have to. I can't take this away from her. After everything I've put Hanna through, I can't be the asshole who destroys this for her.

Before she can argue with me about how impossible the situation is, my phone rings. "That's probably important, since everyone knows you're busy," Hanna says, sliding off my lap to let me answer. I nod, pulling the phone from my pocket.

"Simon, what's wrong?" I ask, not bothering to greet my friend.

"I hate to interrupt, but I was going to leave you a message. I know you're with Hanna, and she needs you. The situation is under control, but I didn't want you to hear it from someone else," he starts.

"Spit it out, Simon," I order.

A moment later, Carrie's voice comes through the phone. "Give me that. I'll tell him, you chicken shit." I'm certain that was directed at Simon, then she speaks to me. "Like he said, it's under control. But The Diner is gone. Someone set it on fire last night. It's a complete loss; there's nothing you can do right now, so don't worry about it. Take care of your Omega."

"I'll be there in thirty," I say, hanging up before she can argue. I turn to my pack. "Looks like the bakery will have a chance for a comeback after all. The Diner is gone. I have to go, but I'll keep you updated."

Hanna grabs my arm. "No. We're going with you. You're not dealing with this alone." I pull her into my arms, holding her close.

"Are you sure? After everything I've done to fuck this up, you really want to be with me right now?" I can't stop myself from asking the question.

She kisses me tenderly. "You still owe me answers. And apologies. But yes, I want to be there. The Diner was your father's dream, just like the bakery was my father's. I want to help you any way I can."

Her words nearly break me. I wipe the tears from my eyes and nod. "Okay. We should go." Leo grabs my keys and we all pile into my SUV. It takes far too long to get there, and when we park, my jaw drops. Carrie was not joking when she said it's a complete loss.

"It's really gone. All of it," I breathe, unable to get out of the car. Hanna gets out and comes over to my door, climbs on my lap and closes the door. She wraps her arms around me and holds on as if I'll disappear.

WILL

There's nothing I can do for my brother right now. I'm forced to watch as he says goodbye to the business our father built from the ground up. The place we spent summers bussing tables. Where we had holiday celebrations and birthday parties that included half the town.

Watching memories go up in smoke isn't easy. Remy can't force himself out of the SUV, and I can't blame him. When

Hanna climbs on Remy's lap, I close the door and follow Leo to talk to the Fire Chief.

I catch myself getting distracted again as they talk about the fire. Then I notice Sam talking to Carrie and Simon. Nodding to Leo, I walk over to see if Sam knows anything we don't. "Carrie, Simon. Sam, anything you can tell me?"

"Not much. It's obvious already that the fire was set, but we don't know what accelerant was used or have any suspects yet. The Fire Marshall has to do his inspection, and hopefully will find something we can use." Sam pauses, clapping a hand on my shoulder. "I'm sorry for your family's loss."

"Me too. But no one was hurt, right? That's the most important thing," I insist. He nods in agreement, and relief washes over me. A building can be replaced, but people can't. That was one of Dad's most important lessons about things like this. I can almost hear his voice in my head, reminding me that it'll all work out. And I know how much worse we would all feel if someone had been injured in this fire.

"I have to get back to the station. I'll give you a call if I learn anything," Sam says before walking away.

Carrie pulls me in for a hug. "We hated interrupting, but figured Remy should know."

"It's okay. Her heat ended sometime late last night. This does change our recovery plan, but it's not your fault. You guys needed to call. He'd have been pissed if someone else had told him before you did," I admit, knowing I'm not telling her anything she doesn't already know.

"I guess we should get out of here; unless there's something you guys need?" Simon offers. I shake my head, but thank him for asking. Watching them walk away, I wonder who could have done this. I know that at some point, Sam will ask us to come in and talk about it at the station. He'll want a list of anyone we think may have been responsible.

My oldest brother isn't the most popular guy in town, but I don't know anyone who would want to hurt him or our family like this. I wipe tears from my face and head back to Remy's car where he and Hanna are still sitting in the passenger seat, holding each other.

A few minutes later, Leo comes back. "Let's go home. Chief is gonna call if they find anything. Insurance should cover everything, once we provide the proof that we didn't do it." He holds up a hand at Hanna's gasp. "It's standard procedure. We have cameras at the front and back door. They'll show me bringing you home, then that we didn't leave again until today, after the fire was nearly out."

LEO

It hurts to see Remy this way. He's so numb that he didn't budge once we got to The Diner. And when we got home, Will and I had to practically carry him back into the house. He isn't talking at all.

"Rem, you have to talk to us," I insist. I'm starting to worry about his mental health. Is he going to do something stupid because of this? Will we lose everything we just gained with the bond? I can't let that happen.

He shakes his head, staring at the wall. At least he's not being violent. I should be happy about that. Instead, I'm terrified that I can't fix this.

"Who would do something like this?" Hanna asks, threading her fingers through Remy's and sitting next to him on the couch.

Will shakes his head. I shrug, unsure what to say. Remy stares stoically at the wall, a single word slipping through his lips. "Sheridan."

"You think Lucas, Jesse, or Bo could have done this?" Hanna covers her mouth with a hand after she asks the question.

Remy shakes his head. "You don't really think Earl did this, do you?" I ask, realizing what he's saying.

"I do," he says with a slow nod, finally turning to look at me. "I have no proof. No one heard him threaten me at The Diner after Hanna's house fire. But that's what it was. A threat. And I'd bet money that he went through with it. I have no idea if he did it himself or paid someone, but I'm sure it was him."

"Why didn't you tell us that he'd threatened you?" Will asks. I don't have to, because I can tell from Remy's expression that he didn't think the old man had it in him.

"If I had considered it a valid threat, I would have," Remy answers, leveling Will with a stare.

"I don't understand," Hanna insists.

Remy pulls her into his lap, banding his arms around her and burying his face in her hair. "I think I do," I say, ready to explain my theory.

"Earl wants the boys to claim Hanna. Lucas told me a while back. Remember? He wanted me to warn him off so he could get the old man off his back," Will says before I have a chance.

I nod my agreement; certain this is exactly what happened. "I don't think his grandsons are as innocent as they appear. Lucas is a stand-up guy, for sure, but Bo and Jesse are the exact type of guys who would do this if Earl told them to.

HANNA

The fact that my guys suspect Mr. Sheridan and his grandsons of setting the fire at The Diner makes my skin crawl. "Do you think that they set the fire at my house, too?" I ask, hoping the answer is no.

Leo nods. "I do. Again, no proof, so we can't just accuse them in public. But it may be worth talking to Sam about. Maybe he'll come here to do it instead of the station."

"I'll give him a call," Will offers. Since he and Sam are close, that's a good idea. If anyone can get Sam to bend the rules, it's Will.

I turn in Remy's arms, wrapping mine around his neck and pulling his head to rest on my shoulder. "Now what?" I ask. With so much uncertainty, I don't know what to say or do to help.

"We wait for the investigation to be complete. Once the insurance pays, we can rebuild," Leo says.

Remy shakes his head. "No. The Diner is gone. It's done. I'm not going to rebuild it. We'll sell the lot and let someone else do something with it."

"But, Remy," I start, but he raises his head and interrupts m e.

"I mean it, Hanna. It's done. Maybe I'll try to convince you to let me come work for you," he says with a sad smile.

"You're hired. Although, I don't think I can afford you," I tease.

"We'll figure it out," he insists. "Even if you can't pay me, I'll still help at the bakery until I figure something else out."

As much as it hurts to see him so defeated, I don't think that's why he's offering to work at the bakery. "We could probably expand the bakery menu a little. Maybe bring in a griddle and do sandwiches?" I offer.

He nods, but doesn't agree the way I expect him to. We could combine our businesses into one, and possibly be successful together. But I don't know if that's what he wants. Would it be so bad to be partners with your Omega? I'm desperate to ask, but terrified of the answer.

I know that in some places, Omegas are considered lesser citizens. In those areas, I wouldn't be able to own a business at all, much less have any say in the running of one. It makes me glad for the small town we live in. Things here have always been better for Omegas. As long as we don't break Pack Law, we're given freedoms most don't have. Which is how I ended up with the bakery when Dad passed.

Mandi and Blake didn't want to run it, but are happy working for me. I love the place, and want to make it successful. I'm just not great at the business part of it.

"I'm serious, Remy. It could work. We'd essentially be combining the bakery and the diner into one business. If we did it right, isn't there a chance it would be better than before?"

TWELVE

Not If It Makes Her Miserable

REMY

I'm too numb right now to consider if Hanna means what she's offering. Seeing The Diner gone broke something inside of me, and I don't know how to fix it. Having Hanna near me is nice, but it's not making me feel any better right now. I've already fucked this up so badly that I'm surprised she wants to be around me, so I keep my mouth shut and let her hold me while she sits on my lap.

When I don't answer her question, she gets quiet. I know that I've offended her, but I can't find the strength to apologize for it. Closing my eyes, I take a deep breath while she strokes my curls off my forehead.

I can't take the pity I'm feeling from her anymore. It's too much. "Hanna, would it be okay if we talked about this later? Today has been a lot, and I'd like to lay down for a while," I say quietly.

"Do you want me to go with you?" she asks, pasting on a sweet smile.

"I think I'd like to be alone for a little while. Spend some time with Leo and Will. I'm okay, really," I attempt to reassure her.

A curt nod is my only response, and I know I've fucked up again. Well, with the diner gone, I'll have plenty of time to make this up to her in the future. She slides off my lap, and I climb the stairs to my room.

I'm careful to close the door quietly. I don't need my brothers coming to jump me because I slammed a door and upset Hanna more. Now that I'm alone, I'm not sure it's what I really want. I just couldn't stand the way they were all looking at me.

I can still smell the smoke on me, even though I didn't get out of the SUV while we were there. A shower. That will help. I lock myself in the bathroom and turn the water on as hot as

I can stand, stepping under it before I allow the tears I've been holding back to fall.

I've let everyone down. Logically, I know the fire isn't my fault. I didn't set it. But this entire situation is still my fault. I caused it when I left a decade ago. The more time passes, the more I realize that things probably would have turned out better if I had stayed instead of running away like I did.

At the time, I hadn't realized that I was running away, but that's exactly what I did. Hanna's father didn't give me the answer I wanted, and I let my pride force me to leave her. I even convinced myself that it was something I did for her. Fuck, I was a stupid kid. There's no use dwelling on the past.

It's too late to change it now. All I can do is move forward and hope that I can find some way to make everything up to Hanna. She deserves so much more than I have to give, especially now.

HANNA

"I shouldn't have pushed him," I say, wiping tears from my cheeks and turning away from Will and Leo.

"He just needs time to process what happened," Leo insists.

"Yeah, don't go easy on him now. He still owes us answers about everything," Will says. They're right, and I know it. But that doesn't make it hurt less that Remy pushed me away again. It's easier to blame myself for it than to admit that I'm scared he's gonna leave me again.

Since we're bonded now, it would be even more miserable if he ran off. The pain of it might kill me. But I can't keep living in fear, can I? I've been on the edge since he came back to town, and that's no way to live. Maybe I should have refused to bond with them during my heat.

"What if this changes how he feels about me? About this pack?" I ask, staring out the window, refusing to meet their eyes.

"Hanna," Leo says, scooting closer. "All three of us are here for you. Yes, Remy has fucked up in the past, but he's not leaving."

I can't force myself to look at him. I want him to be right, but I can't convince myself that Remy will stick around. "How can you be so sure? I never thought he'd leave before, but he did. Without so much as a goodbye or second thought for me. Just because we're bonded, that won't stop him."

I don't need to see his face to know that my words hurt him. As much as I don't want that, it can't be helped right now.

"Well, since we're all bonded now, it wouldn't be as bad if he did," Will says. I glare at him, and he continues. "Yes, it would suck if he left, but it wouldn't destroy the pack. We'd still be good as far as the Council is concerned. That's all I meant."

He makes a good point, but that doesn't make the idea of Remy leaving any less painful than it was the last time. Why did I let this man have the power to destroy me? As if I ever had a choice when it comes to Remy Kerrisk. I shake my head.

"I think I'm gonna go read for a bit. Is my book still in your room?" I ask Leo. When he nods instead of speaking, I head upstairs. I'm surprised when neither of them follows me.

WILL

"I'm gonna kill him," I growl when Hanna leaves the room. "We can't let him get away with destroying her like this again."

"He's suffering right now, Will. We need to give him time and space to feel his emotions and work through the grief. For him, it's kind of like losing Dad all over again. And since he wasn't here with us the first time, I'm sure he's dealing with that guilt too," Leo argues.

When he stands up and moves toward the stairs, I step in front of him. "Where do you think you're going?"

"I'm going to get Hanna a bottle of water and make sure she has everything she needs. Then I'm going to read or watch some TV while everyone calms down," he says, shoving me out of his way. I know he's not angry with me, but I'm still pissed at Remy.

Trying to fight against my urge to storm up to Remy's room and pound my fists into his face until he apologizes to Hanna, I pace the living room for a while. When that doesn't calm me down, I take the stairs two at a time. I pause for a moment outside my brother's door, forcing myself to take deep breaths.

While I'm trying to get my rage under control, the door swings open, and I'm face to face with my oldest brother. Remy's chest heaves the same way mine does. "What do you want?" he asks with a growl.

"I want you to stop being an immature ass who keeps hurting our Omega," I answer, slamming my fist into his face. As he stumbles backward into his bedroom, I follow, fists raised again. I expect him to fight back. I'm prepared for this to get ugly.

What I'm not prepared for is him to hold up his hands in surrender. "You're right. I deserved that. But it's the only free shot you're gonna get," he says. "I didn't mean to hurt Hanna. My intentions don't mean much, I know. I was about to go find her and talk when you surprised me."

"Seriously?" I ask, shocked. Remy has never admitted that anyone else could be right about anything.

"Look, I don't expect you to understand. I've made lots of mistakes, and I needed to grow up. I'm working on that now. I'll talk to you and Leo after I fix things with Hanna," he says.

LEO

When I walk away from Will, I know that he's going to end up fighting Remy over this. Our youngest brother has a temper, and he's not very good at controlling it. Especially where Hanna is concerned. After Remy left us, Will wanted to follow him to Chicago and beat him up then. Our father barely talked him out of it.

Without Dad here to stop him, I know there's nothing I can do to keep it from happening. So, I focus on our Omega instead of the Alpha hormones that are escalating toward violence.

I check her nest first, and when Hanna's not there, I grab a bottle of water from the mini fridge. Since she's not in her space, I know exactly where I'll find her. I ease the door to my room open, freezing in the doorway when she jumps. "It's just me. I brought you some water. Do you need anything else?" I ask
.

Her eyes are red and her cheeks are flushed. She's been crying. Fuck. Now I want to hit Remy. *Deep breaths, Leo.* "I'm okay," she says quietly.

I walk into the room and place the bottle of water on the nightstand next to her. "I'll leave you alone, then," I offer, starting toward the door.

"Don't go," she pleads. My heart warms and I continue toward the door, closing it softly. Then I cross the room and scoop her into my arms.

"Whatever you need, I'm here," I say, pressing a kiss to her temple.

"I just don't want to be alone. Will you hold me for a while?" Her words break something in me. I nod, pulling her close and snuggling into the covers with her. I'm pretty sure she'll fall asleep soon, but I don't tell her that. I know her well enough to know that she'll fight it.

"Do you want to watch something?" I ask, settling her against my side with her head resting on my chest. She hums in approval. I grab the remote and turn on her favorite movie, knowing that it's what she watches when she's upset.

Hanna's breathing slows and I'm certain she's almost asleep when I hear a commotion from the direction of Remy's room. That would be Will. I look down at the sleeping Omega, surprised that she didn't wake up. I'm not moving her to get in the middle of their scuffle. Hopefully they don't break anything.

A moment later, the noise stops. I can't help wondering if Will knocked Remy out. I shift in the bed a little, but Hanna holds tightly to my shirt. That makes my decision for me; I'm not going anywhere. If they need something, one of them can come in here.

REMY

I wasn't expecting Will's right hook when I opened the door and found him standing there. The most surprising thing about it was that it didn't happen sooner. I know he's pissed at me for leaving, and for coming back. I think part of his issue is that Dad's gone, and he doesn't know how to process that.

"I don't think Hanna wants to talk to you right now," he says, blocking the door.

"What makes you say that?" I ask. "Did she say something?"

"Yeah, that she thinks you'll leave again," he mutters.

"I'm not going anywhere. Did you tell her that?" I can't stand the fact that I've ruined Hanna's ability to trust me. But surely, my brothers would defend me to her, wouldn't they?

"I didn't. But Leo did. She's not convinced," he shrugs. "So, she went to his room to be alone. Then he went to check on her. Since his door is closed and I haven't seen him, I'm pretty sure he's still in there with her."

I nod. "Okay, I'll give her some time to calm down. And I'll find a way to prove to her that I'm not going anywhere. Because I'm not leaving again." I say the words with as much conviction as I can. I'm not planning on leaving Echo Falls again unless my pack comes with me. And they're pretty content here, so I don't think it'll ever happen.

Will seems satisfied with that answer. His posture relaxes a little. "Why did you leave? I know you want to talk to Hanna about it first, but I'm here now, and I want answers."

I nod, gesturing toward the bed. "You wanna sit? We can talk about it."

He walks over and flops on my bed, waiting for me to talk. When I don't, he raises his eyebrows. "Let's talk, then."

Taking a deep breath, I tell my youngest brother the story of the worst day of my life. I'm careful to include details that didn't hit me at the time. I even give him the parts of the story that make me the bad guy. Because that's what I am here. I'm the asshole who left when I should have stayed.

"And that's what happened. It all boils down to a misunderstanding by an immature kid who didn't want to face the fact that he wasn't ready for what he wanted. So, I ran away. I convinced myself that it was the best thing for everyone. I was wrong," I admit when I'm finished with my story.

"Fuck, Rem. You should have talked to us about it. Leo and I would have helped you see that you were taking that all wrong. We could have worked together to be ready sooner instead of waiting a decade for you to come home," Will says. His anger has subsided, but I'm not sure I deserve his forgiveness.

"I know. But at the time, it seemed like the only way. And by the time I realized that I'd made a huge mistake, I was halfway through culinary school. I couldn't leave without finishing. Then it was too late. I'd expected to come home and find Hanna claimed by another pack," I say, rubbing a hand over my chest, trying to ease the ache there at the memories.

"So, what was the deal with you getting upset when Hanna offered to share the bakery? It seems like a good idea, at least temporarily. If you're gonna rebuild, it would help until the new diner is done," he says.

I shake my head. "I'm not rebuilding. I meant that. The Diner isn't my dream. It was Dad's, and I was happy to keep it alive as long as I could. And if Hanna takes some time to think about it, then decides that she wants me as a partner at the bakery, I'll accept. I don't want her to make snap decisions like that without considering everything first. That business is her father's legacy, and it deserves to be preserved."

"Then what is your dream?" Will asks. It's a tough question that I've been asking myself for a while.

"You know how I made all those changes to the menu at the diner?" I ask in return. He nods. "That's what I want. I'd be much happier working at the bakery with Hanna than I was at The Diner. But I won't push that on her."

"But if it's what would make you happy, isn't that what you should do?"

"Not if it makes her miserable," I answer.

HANNA

I wake in Leo's arms, realizing that I've missed most of the movie. "It's okay, buttercup, we can watch it again later. You needed the rest."

His amaretto scent surrounds me, comforting and warm. But my heart aches, and I know that I'm going to have to talk to Remy before the pain will subside. My eyes meet Leo's, and I can see that he already knows what I'm going to say. "I have no idea if he's conscious. After you fell asleep, I'm pretty sure Will went in there and they fought. Then it got really quiet. I can come with you, if you want," he offers.

I shake my head. "No, I need to do this myself. I'll yell if I need help." I press a soft kiss to his lips and enjoy the hug he gives me before he drops his arms from around me.

A moment later, I'm standing outside Remy's room, raising my hand to knock, when the door swings open. Will spins me around, kissing me hard. "Try to go easy on him. He's a dumbass," he says, setting me down inside the room and pulling the door closed as he leaves.

I turn around, and Remy is looking at me. "Hi," he says.

"Hi," I answer. "Do you think we could talk?"

He nods, patting the bed next to him. As much as I don't want to be that close to him, I walk across the room and stand in front of him. "It's okay that you're still mad at me. I am too," he offers, putting his hands on my hips.

I step closer, resting my hands on his shoulders. "I'm mad, but it's more than that. I'm hurt, Remy. It feels like you didn't trust me back then, and that you still don't now. What did I do wrong?"

His jaw drops and his eyes go wide. "What did you do wrong? Hanna, you never did anything wrong. It was me; it was always me."

"But you didn't even say goodbye," I insist, fighting against the quiver of my lip and holding back the tears that fill my eyes.

Remy pulls me even closer, resting his head on my chest and wrapping his arms around me. "Hanna, I am so sorry. I owe you more than just those words, and I know it. I will spend the rest of my life making this up to you."

Then he tells me the story of how an eighteen-year-old kid asked my father for permission to court me and got turned down, then ran away instead of facing his fears.

Stay Close

REMY

Hanna listens quietly as I explain my story. I know that no matter how many times I apologize, I can't go back and change the past. Our history is what it is, and has the potential to tear us apart. When I'm finished, she doesn't speak. I wait a while to give her time to process what I've said.

"Will you say something?" I can't take the silence anymore, and she isn't even looking at me.

Her eyes meet mine, and I see the tears shining there. "Oh, Remy. I had no idea. You should have just told me. We could have figured it out together."

I nod, shame and guilt taking hold of me again. "I wanted to prove to him that I was good enough, even though he never actually said I wasn't. I was a kid, and it was all a huge misunderstanding. If you can't forgive me, I'll understand."

"If you pull away from me again, I will get both of your brothers to throttle you. Or to hold you down while I do," she says, grabbing my face in both of her hands. "We've lost so much time already. I can't promise not to get upset with you when you act like an ass. But I'm not going anywhere."

Hanna captures my lips with hers in a desperate kiss. It's not what I expected, but it's exactly what I need. I drag her body closer to me and she shoves me back. Giving her the one thing I can in this moment is easy, so I let her have control. This Omega could do whatever she wanted to me, and I would let her. Even if it destroyed me.

She keeps kissing me while I'm lying on my back with her on my chest. I could get lost in her so easily. Her maple cinnamon scent is sweet and enticing, surrounding me in nothing but her.

When she stops and sits up on me, breaking all contact except for where she's sitting, I gasp for breath. "What's wrong?" I ask.

"I just remembered why I was so mad at you before my heat. And before anything else happens, we're going to sort that out," she says, crossing her arms over her chest.

I take a deep breath, understanding that there's no way to avoid this conversation, either. But maybe she'll let me explain. "Can I explain myself first? Or do you want to yell at me?" I ask.

"What's there to explain? You decided to sell my family home without even talking to me about it first," she growls. It's the cutest sound ever, but I keep that thought to myself. There's no point in making her angrier by pointing out that she's adorable when she's mad.

"If you'll let me, I think I can." I wait a beat for her to argue, then continue when she doesn't. "It was wrong of me to make that decision without talking to you about it first. I'm sorry for that. But I think when you find out who I want to sell it to, you'll agree it's the perfect idea," I offer, holding my hands up in surrender.

Hanna takes a shaky breath. "Who do you want to sell it to?" she asks, barely audible.

"Blake," I answer with a smirk. "He asked me about it that day, and I approached the whole thing wrong. I should have asked you instead of telling you. You're right, it's *your* family home, and you should be the one to decide what happens to it. In my defense, I thought you'd be on board with selling it to your brother for a fair but low price, giving you some money to invest in the bakery. Since you'll be living here with your pack now. I hope."

"You're such an ass. I should hate you," she says, wiping tears from her cheeks. I want to kiss them away, but I know I can't do that yet. I also know that if she stays where she is, we're going to have something else to discuss. The heat of her core presses against my cock, and it's starting to respond.

"But you don't. You love me," I tease, hoping that this means she's going to forgive me for this much at least.

"We should sell it to Blake. I would have just given it to him. But you were thinking about how to help me with the bakery. It's sweet, especially since you're the reason I was losing business," she says.

"I never meant to cause that. I was just trying to make The Diner my own. As usual, I never considered how my actions would hurt you," I admit.

She leans over and presses a kiss to my lips. "You're gonna have to do better with that. We're a pack now, and you are the one in charge. You have to think about what's best for everyone, not just you."

"I know. I'm trying. And I have you to keep me on track, so I think I'll be okay," I answer with a smirk.

"Well, that's two of the things we needed to discuss. Let's tackle the third while we're still getting along," she insists.

I'm not sure what she's talking about. What else could we have to discuss? I scrunch my face in confusion, making her laugh.

"Why don't you want me to make changes at the bakery to incorporate part of the diner?" she asks, her smile falling.

"I don't want to take over your business, or your father's legacy, with mine. Besides, The Diner was never my dream," I answer, finally giving her the truth she's been seeking. I know now that I have to be honest with her or risk losing her. Since we're bonded, I know how badly losing her would hurt her. I'm not worried about my pain, but I'll do what I can to prevent hers.

"So, you don't want to work at the bakery with me?" The sadness in her voice destroys me.

"No, cupcake, it's not that. I would be honored to work at the bakery with you. I just don't want you to change it for me. If those changes were something you'd wanted before I came back to town, fine, but I don't think they were," I explain.

"Then you'll come work with me while the diner is rebuilt?"

I shake my head. "I meant it when I said I'm not rebuilding. The Diner is done. But I would love to come work with you, if you'll have me."

"Are you sure?" she asks. I pull her down to me and kiss her like she's the one thing I need to live. Maybe she is.

"I'm sure," I say when I finally break the kiss.

HANNA

I'm floored by how honest Remy is being with me about everything. In one hour, I've learned more about him than I knew ten years ago. It hurts me that he's not going to rebuild his father's diner, but if I want him to let me decide what happens to my family home, I have to trust him to make that same decision about his family's property.

I lean over him, kissing lazily along his jaw. His fresh citrus scent hits me, and I know that my panties are soaked. It was nearly impossible to finish our conversation when his dick started to harden under me. But we needed to get things cleared up. And now that we have, I can take what I want. If he lets me have control long enough.

His fingers thread into my hair, lightly scratching against my scalp. Tingles shoot down my spine, and I grind my core against his growing length. A nervous laugh escapes me when he flips me over, taking control.

"Hey," I protest. "I was doing something there."

"Yes, you were driving me crazy. Now it's my turn," he says, kissing my neck near his bond mark. I turn my head, giving him better access. I don't mind that he's taking control back from me. I think I'll enjoy letting Remy boss me around for a b it.

The only time I've been intimate with any of my mates was during my heat, since it happened so soon after the contract was approved. I expect Remy to be controlling and dominating. When he kisses me tenderly and gently runs his hands along my body, I'm caught off guard. A shiver runs down my spine and I shake it off.

"We don't have to," he says, pausing.

I wrap my legs around him, locking my ankles together. "If you don't, I'll go get one of your brothers to come in here and take care of me, while the other one holds you down and makes you watch." It's an empty threat, but he doesn't need to know that. Another rejection from Remy might destroy me, and that wouldn't be something I would turn to his brothers to fix.

He play growls at me, then drags my shirt over my head. The moment he realizes I'm not wearing a bra; his eyes go wide. "You are so beautiful," he whispers, peeling my pants and panties off.

For a moment, I'm self-conscious at being naked in front of him when I'm not being controlled by my heat. But the way he looks at me eases any nerves I had. Remy looks ravenous, staring at me as if I'm his next meal. I have to admit, it's a powerful feeling.

I watch as he tosses his clothes to the side, not giving me the chance to strip him the way he did me. I'm almost disappointed at that, until his mouth trails up my thigh, aiming for my core. Slick pools between my legs.

Remy's lips brush against my sex, teasing, tasting. He hums in approval, and dives in devouring me. He laps at my slick, his tongue brushing against my opening before zeroing in on my clit. The way his tongue flicks and caresses sends me over the edge faster than I've ever fallen.

He raises up, climbing my body as he presses his mouth to my skin, kissing, nipping, and licking a path up to my lips. His kiss is possessive, and I can taste my release on him.

I arch my hips, coating his cock in my slick. Remy's breath hitches, and he groans. I know I'm about to get exactly what I want. Then, without warning, he slams into me, fully seating himself in one stroke. Without the haze of my heat distracting me, I can feel every move.

Each slide of his skin against mine as he thrusts into me over and over inches me closer to another orgasm. The way he worships my body drives me crazy. Remy has never been gentle or sweet, but he's being both of those now. Instead of fucking me how I'd expected, he makes love to me, ensuring I know how he feels about me. It's not a feral drive toward release, but a steady, slow build that is both glorious and torturous at the same time.

When I finally let go, the orgasm takes me, and I cry out my release. I feel Remy's knot swell inside me, and his release follows mine. For a moment, I consider how drastically our lives have changed since my Alpha came back. Not all of it has been good, but it seems to be working out. How many more changes are in store for us?

At some point, we'll have to discuss all the options for our future, but now is not that time. I want to have those moments with these men, learning what they want from life, and how they plan to chase after it. Planning for a family and possibly expanding the bakery are my biggest desires. Both can wait for now. We still have time to figure those out after we spend some time getting to know each other again.

Everyone changes, especially after ten years apart. I know that we need to spend some time together as a pack before we start talking about having kids or expanding my business. And I'm sure each of my men will have an opinion about both. For now, I relax into Remy's arms, letting him hold me as he gently rocks against me.

LEO

Hanna needs to talk to Remy, and I support that decision. I hate that she has to do it on her own, but I understand her need for answers. I want them too, but this situation is bigger than me. Our Omega needs to know that her Alpha isn't going to abandon her again. I stand in the doorway as she approaches his room.

Her hesitation to knock grips my heart like a vice. I want to erase every bit of pain he's caused her. There's no way to do that, so I have to let them move forward however they can. I just hope that involves the four of us being a family.

The door jerks open and Will twirls her, then deposits her inside the room and closes the door. "What the fuck was that about?" I ask him.

"Rem and I talked it out. After I sucker punched him. There's a lot we didn't know, and he admitted that most of it was his stupidity. I'm sure he'll tell you about it later," he offers.

"You sucker punched him and he didn't fight back?"

Will shakes his head. "Nope. But he did tell me I only got one free shot. Since he started talking after that, I didn't push my luck."

"Do you think they'll be okay?" I gesture at the door, wondering if Hanna's suspicions about Remy leaving again are warranted.

"He's not going anywhere. If they're not okay, it's because she won't forgive him. I don't think it's gonna be an easy road for any of us, but they can get through it. As long as he's honest with her the way he was with me, I think she'll give him a chance to make it up to her."

I exchange a look with my brother. "When did you get so mature? You're supposed to be the baby," I laugh.

"We all had to grow up faster once Remy left. You know that," he counters. And he's not wrong. When Remy left us, Dad pushed his responsibilities onto us. I would have taken it all on myself, but I'm not an Alpha, so there were certain things I couldn't handle without causing problems with the Council.

"I know. I guess I'm gonna make some calls and check on everything, since Hanna and Remy are okay for now. Will you stay close enough to step in if she needs you?"

Will nods. "I'm not sensing anything bad along the bond, besides her frustration with him. If things go sideways, I'll break the door down and take him out. Just make sure everything else is still standing. I'd hate for something else to happen today."

I agree with him on that. Heading downstairs to my office, I pull out my phone and send texts out to check on the bakery and the bar. I'll let Will reach out to Sam about our suspicions. Once I'm settled in the office, I check my email, going over the payroll submissions from Maisy and approving them for the bar and the bakery.

It may be overstepping, and Hanna may get upset with me, but when she went into heat, I asked Maisy to send me whatever our girl usually handled. There was no way for her to sign off on payroll or scheduling while she was in heat. Since neither Mandi nor Blake actually wanted to run the bakery, I figured they'd get irritated at having to deal with things outside of their usual.

Blake texts me back to let me know the bakery is doing well. Business picked up today because of the fire, so they had to call Henry and Simon in to help out.

Then Jasper lets me know that the bar has been steady, but that he had to send Simon to help at the bakery because he couldn't get away. And since I'm still not available to go in tonight, Simon will cover my shift at the bar after he finishes at the bakery.

We really have the best friends anyone could ask for. I make a note to have a thank you party once everything is settled here. Our friends have gone above and beyond while we've been tied up with Hanna's heat, and then today with the fire.

With that taken care of, I call the firehouse to see if anyone has an update. "Hey, Leo," Jason Conley says smoothly when he answers.

"Hey, J. You got an update for me?"

"No word yet. They won't let any of us near it, since we finally got the fire out. Dad's got the state inspector coming in because he doesn't trust Sheridan to do the investigation," he explains. Jason's father is the Sheriff, and I'd nearly forgotten that Earl Sheridan was the fire investigator for Echo Falls.

"So, he already knows about the threats, then?" I don't bother to hide anything, since Jason admitted the Sheriff doesn't trust Sheridan either.

"Yeah. People were talking. Carrie overheard Sheridan talking to Remy the other day. She wasn't quiet about it when Sheridan tried to push his way into the investigation. I'm glad she was there, or he might have been able to mess something up. Dad's not saying he's a suspect, but the fact that people heard him threaten Remy means he can't be the one to investigate," Jason explains.

"Good. But they're for sure calling it arson?" I ask, already knowing the answer.

"Can confirm. We're just waiting for the state guy to come in and give us the details. Dad would have let us check out the scene further, but Sheridan threw a fit when he wasn't allowed to touch anything. Said it would be easy for any of us to plant something to frame him because we're your friends. Can you imagine that? Like we'd plant evidence," Jason scoffs.

"What an asshole. I'm sorry, man. Thanks for letting me know what's going on. I'll talk to you later," I say before disconnecting the call.

Fourteen

Drop the Alpha Bullshit

WILL

True to my word, I settle in my room where I can almost hear what's going on in Remy's. While it should disturb me, it's actually comforting, because I know that he's taking care of her for once. I'm relieved that my oldest brother has finally found someone he wants to put first. Especially since she's my

Omega, too. I'm certain our pack is going to come through this stronger than ever.

When my phone buzzes with a text, I check it while keeping my ears open for signs of Hanna being in trouble.

SAM: *Did old man Sheridan really threaten Remy at The Diner?*

I laugh, wondering how he's already heard about this.

ME: *He did. Who told you?*

SAM: *Carrie, and a few regulars who claim to have overheard him.*

Well, I guess I don't have to call him with our suspicions now, if Carrie and others reported the threats.

ME: *Are you looking into him, then?*

I already know he won't be able to tell me much about the case.

SAM: *He's a person of interest now, yeah. The state inspector is coming in to handle the investigation, since Sheridan is possibly compromised.*

Good. I'm glad they're not gonna let the old man get away with setting this fire and then brushing it under the rug. Of course, he could have just had someone set the fire for him. We don't know yet exactly what happened. Hopefully we'll get answers soon.

Since I don't have to call Sam, and Hanna seems okay with Remy—there are no negative emotions bouncing around on the bond right now—I decide to check my email and see how my business is holding up to my impromptu vacation.

I have a couple of emails confirming that customers were happy to wait, since Maisy let them know the situation. Then there are a few canceling orders. Well, that's unfortunate, but to be expected. Some people don't know how to be patient. I respond to the ones that need answers, then email confirmation of cancellations.

With my work settled until I go back tomorrow morning, I head downstairs for a sandwich. I pause for a moment outside Remy's door. It doesn't sound like they're fighting or killing each other, so I decide food is okay.

HANNA

By the time Remy's knot goes down, I realize that we missed lunch. "We should get something to eat," I suggest, still sprawled across his chest.

"Probably a good idea, at least so my brothers don't think you've killed me," he teases. I swat his arm.

"I think they're more worried about you hurting me than the other way around," I admit. I wince when pain shows in his eyes. "I didn't mean that the way it sounded."

He smiles and shakes his head. "They're not wrong. I am more likely to hurt you than you are to hurt me. Because you are the most perfect Omega that ever existed."

He presses a kiss to my forehead before easing out from under me to get dressed. "Let's get you something to eat, shall we?" Remy hands me my discarded panties and pants, then pulls his shirt over my head. "Much better."

I don't argue, because I love being surrounded by their scents. Normally, Leo makes sure I have something that smells like each of them, so it's nice when Remy does this for me. "Thank you," I say, raising up on my toes to kiss his cheek.

He tosses on a pair of sweatpants and threads his fingers through mine, pulling me toward the door. I'm worried that he's gonna drag me down the stairs, but he slows down when we get closer.

We find Will and Leo in the kitchen making sandwiches. "We were considering bringing you guys something to eat," Leo says, handing me a plate. Will surprises me by handing his plate to Remy. A few minutes later, we're all sitting around the table eating together. With everything that's happened the past couple of weeks, it should feel awkward, but it doesn't.

"Everything has been a lot lately, huh?" I say, digging into my sandwich.

"Yeah, we missed the baking competition, claimed our girl, and lost the diner all in a week," Remy answers. I can't stop the way I flinch at his words. I know he wasn't trying to blame me for missing the contest, but it is my fault.

"I'm sorry," I offer.

He shakes his head. "It wouldn't have been as much fun without you anyway." His response is not at all what I expected.

"But I'd already backed out, so you would have been doing it all without me anyway," I insist.

"You'd think so, but that's not how it was gonna go," he smirks.

"What are you talking about?" I ask.

"I might have rescinded your withdrawal from the contest, with Mayor Barry's help," he laughs. I slap his arm. Wait, didn't he say something about this earlier? With the fire, I completely forgot!

"You asshole! Why would you do that?"

Will laughs. "He didn't want you to give up just because he was a dick." Leave it to Remy to do something completely inappropriate as an apology.

"I can't believe she would let you do that. You can't make that decision for me," I argue.

"She let me arrange for us to be paired up, didn't she?"

My eyes go wide. "She what? You mean you were behind all of that?" He winces at my tone. "How? Why? I don't understand," I say.

"What can I say? Mayor Barry is a sucker for love. She was willing to do whatever she could to put us together so you'd eventually forgive me," he smirks. "I know I shouldn't have done it, but it's done now."

REMY

I'm shocked at how well Hanna is taking all of this. Finding out that I've been pulling the strings for the Founder's Day events where we were shoved together can't be easy.

"Okay, you're right. It doesn't matter now. Especially since we both missed the contest. I wonder who won," Hanna says.

"Maisy's grandma, same as last year," Leo says. "She told me in the emails she sent about payroll."

Hanna's eyes go wide. "Shit. I need to check my email. I have to approve my payroll and overtime so everyone gets paid."

Leo makes a face. "I already did. I had Maisy send me everything when you went into heat, so that you didn't have to stress over it. How mad are you?"

I don't blame my brother for worrying about upsetting Hanna. She's very independent, and likes to be in control.

She laughs, and my jaw drops. Hanna laughs at Leo making decisions for her. She got pissed when I did it, but it's okay for him? "What the fuck?" I ask.

"I know, I should be mad. But if I'm forgiving you for being that way, I can't exactly yell at him for the same thing. I know you guys are just trying to take care of me. Even if I don't necessarily approve of your methods, I get why you did it this time. We'll have a better plan in place for my next heat," Hanna says.

And just like that, any potential argument is over. I want to be annoyed, but I'm just glad she's not upset. "Also, Remy, I know you don't understand this, but Leo doing that to help me is not the same as you making decisions for me when you know I want my opinion to be heard."

Ah, there it is. At least I understand why it was different for him than for me. "Fair enough," I agree, finishing my sandwich.

"What do we need to do to deal with the fire?" I ask, knowing that Leo has probably already talked to someone at the firehouse.

"Jason says the state inspector is coming down to do the investigation. Sheriff has decided that Sheridan is a person of interest, and the old man showed his ass a little, so now no one local can touch anything without it looking suspicious," Leo explains.

"So, we'll wait. Which means we won't be able to get things cleaned up for a while. I guess that frees me up to go to the bakery with you in the morning, if you're still interested in that," I say, turning to Hanna.

She nods. "I would love that."

"Good. That's one thing settled. I think getting back to our routines will be good for all of us. And before anyone else asks, no, I'm not rebuilding The Diner. I meant that. I'm gonna work with Hanna at the bakery for a while, and see if something else interests me," I say.

"What about your employees?" Will asks.

"Well, a few of them pick up shifts at the bar and the bakery anyway. The others will have to find other jobs. I'll send out texts this afternoon to let people know. I doubt any of them will be shocked by the news," I answer.

LEO

Remy's plan seems solid. Getting back to our normal lives will be nice. But losing the diner has to be painful for him. It's like losing Dad all over again, or at least, that's how it feels to me. I'm not sure how he or Will are staying so calm about it.

As if she can read my mind, Hanna reaches for my hand. "It's not gonna be easy, and it's gonna hurt for a while. But we'll get through it."

"Thanks. I needed to hear that," I answer. I can't help wondering if Sheridan really is the one behind the fires. If he is, what's he gonna do next? Will he come after Hanna directly, or just keep setting our properties on fire?

"I think we need a plan of action for how to handle things with Sheridan, or whoever is doing this," Will says. "This shit has cost me a couple of commission jobs, and I'm not thrilled about it."

"We can't do anything. We have to let the cops and state inspector do their jobs. If they decide that he's to blame for the fires, he'll get arrested," I say. It may not be easy to keep my hot-headed brother from retaliating, but I have to try. I can't let this devolve into a tit-for-tat situation.

"But how are we gonna protect ourselves?" he asks. "We can't just go on like we're not in danger. What if someone attacks Hanna?"

"I understand that concern, but we have to do what we usually do. We have to let the authorities handle it. We can't go rogue here. I'd rather not end up in jail for retaliating against someone only to find out that they weren't actually responsible," I argue.

"You really think he had nothing to do with this?" Will argues.

"No one is saying that Sheridan is innocent, Will. We're just not condoning an attack against him when we have no proof that he did this. Of course, we need to take precautions. It's probably not safe for any of us to be alone unless we're in a public place with lots of witnesses," Hanna says.

Her idea makes sense, but I'm not sure how she'll get Will to agree. He usually works at his shop alone. And sometimes she works at the bakery by herself too. "How are we gonna manage to pair up?" I ask, trying to understand her idea.

"Well, if Remy is working with me, that takes care of us. Jasper is with you most of the day, so you're basically covered, too. That just leaves Will. Who can we get to help you in your shop so that you're not alone?" Hanna asks.

Will scoffs. "I'll be fine on my own. I'm worried about keeping you three safe."

HANNA

I expect Remy to be difficult about this, but he seems to be the least bothered by the fact that I want us not to be alone. Why is Will trying to fight me on this?

"Well, I'm worried about you," I insist. "If you won't let me find someone to hang out with you, then I'll have Sam stop by or send an officer to check on you while you're at the shop."

He glares at me, and for a moment, I wonder if his temper is worse than Remy's. I get my answer a moment later when he explodes at me. "Why are you treating me like I'm a child? I am a full-grown Alpha, and I will not allow my Omega to dictate where I can go and who I need to have around me."

Shit. I wasn't expecting that reaction. "I wasn't treating you like a child. Someone is trying to hurt my family, and I'm terrified. I just want to know that you're safe."

"I don't need a babysitter. I can handle myself. I'm done with this conversation," he argues, standing up to leave. It's nice to know that his temper hasn't improved with age. Will has always been a bit of a hot head.

"Will," Remy growls.

Will rounds on him. "No. You will not pull the Pack Alpha card on me now. You have no right. Just because you explained why you left and admitted that it was stupid, that doesn't mean we're all just going to accept that your word is law now. You have to earn our respect, brother. I'll see you all tomorrow. I can't stay here right now."

Before I can make a move to try and stop him, Will storms out of the house. My heart races, my hands tremble, and a thin bead of sweat trails down the back of my neck. I have no way to know that he's going to be safe out there, and I don't know how to deal with how scared I am for all of us.

Tears start to fall, and Remy pulls me into his arms. "I can go after him, if that will make you feel better," he offers.

Leo clears his throat. "I think it would be better if I went. He's pretty pissed at you right now, and if you go, it'll just end up in a fight. At least if I go, there's a chance he won't swing at me."

"I don't like the idea of either of you being out there alone," I admit. "But I understand why you should go instead of Remy." Leo kisses me gently before he heads out to find Will and try to talk some sense into him.

Once he's gone, I turn in Remy's arms. "Do you think I overstepped as your Omega?"

He shakes his head. "No, cupcake. It was a reasonable request given the situation. And you weren't treating him like a child. He was acting like one, though."

"I can't help feeling that he's right. I know I don't act like a normal Omega. And I'm aware that our dynamics have changed a little since high school. Knowing that someone is out to hurt you guys is too much for me. I can't handle it," I admit.

Remy presses a kiss to my temple. "Will was out of line; not you. You didn't demand anything from him. You asked that we make adjustments to ensure our safety. It was not unreasonable. Please don't let him convince you that you are a bad Omega because he threw a fit in response to your request."

"I'll try. I don't know how to handle his anger, though. Will's never been mad at me before," I say.

"It'll blow over pretty quickly. He's got a short temper, but he doesn't hold on to it for long. I'm sure Leo will talk him out of it," Remy insists.

I hope he's right. I can't stand the idea that Will thinks I tried to control him. That wasn't my intention at all. Somehow, I'd expected him to understand my fear. But I guess if he doesn't feel it too, he couldn't really get it.

WILL

I'm not sure what makes Hanna think I can't take care of myself anymore. Her insistence that we're not safe is ridiculous. Yeah, some asshole started a couple of fires. That doesn't mean that they're out to hurt us. So far, it's just been some property damage. Okay, a lot of property damage.

But I'm an Alpha, and that makes me stronger than my Omega. It's my job to protect her, not the other way around. And Remy trying to push his opinion on me just made things worse. I can't let my family think I'm weak.

I pace the floor in my workshop, trying to stomp off the anger. I know I probably overreacted, but I can't seem to get past the idea that my Omega is trying to tell me what I can and can't do. Maybe my brothers are okay with that, but I'm not.

I'm not one of those guys who thinks an Omega's place is barefoot and pregnant, but that doesn't mean that she should be the one in charge, either. If Remy wants to be Pack Alpha, he needs to figure out how to get Hanna to ease up on controlling us.

When the door swings open and Leo walks in, I jump. Maybe I'm a little nervous about the situation after all. "Did Hanna send you after me?"

"No. I offered to come, because I didn't think you and Remy should be alone together right now. I don't need you killing our Pack Alpha because you got your panties in a twist," Leo says.

"Fuck you," I growl.

"Nah, I'm good. You're not my type, little brother. And you can drop the Alpha bullshit with me. I know you're just as scared as she is. So why don't you want someone to hang out with you? Do you just like knowing that Hanna's so worried she can't function?" he replies.

"What? I never said I like her being worried. I just don't want someone telling me what to do," I argue.

"Except she wasn't telling you what to do. She just asked that we all take more precautions to stay safe," Leo says.

FIFTEEN

On Our Own

LEO

I STARE AT MY little brother, shaking my head. He's still trying to argue about Hanna's simple request that we keep each other safe. It's ridiculous. When he doesn't respond, I continue.

"So, you'd rather ruin your relationship with your pack than let a friend come hang out with you while you work?" I ask.

"I didn't say that, Leo. I just don't want someone telling me what to do," he argues.

"I know. You keep saying that. But how do you expect her to want to be with you if you don't respect her?" This argument is pointless, and I'm just about to give up.

"Do you really think she'd decide that she didn't want me over this?" he asks, going quiet for a while. I wonder if I'm finally starting to get through to him.

"Would you blame her if she did?" I counter. I'm tempted to go home and leave him here by himself, except that would be the opposite of why I came. And I don't want Hanna to worry any more than she has to.

So, instead of walking away, I turn away from him and pull a chair over by the open bay door. If he wants to be an ass, I'll babysit. For now. I pull out my phone and send a quick text letting Hanna know that we're okay. Then I spend a few minutes scrolling social media while my brother stews in what I've said to him.

I don't react when the bench sander comes on. Honestly, I fully expect him to work on something since he's here, and he's pissed. Maybe it'll help him figure out what he wants. I expected Remy to have issues bonding with Hanna, but I guess I should have been more worried about Will and his temper.

Watching them suffer over something stupid doesn't work for me. I'll convince him that he's being a pig-headed asshole one way or another. I shift my chair so I can keep an eye on him while he works.

WILL

Stupid fucking bastard. Dickhead Beta. How dare he say those things to me? If he wasn't my older brother, I'd have half a mind to beat his ass. Does he want Hanna to abandon me because of this argument?

When he turns his back on me and drags one of my chairs over to the bay doors, I decide that I need to get some work done. If I don't, I'll end up punching him. And as angry as I am right now, I don't think hitting Leo will make me feel better.

I sand down the legs for the table I'm building, even though it's one of the canceled orders. The damned thing was more than half done when they sent the email to cancel. So, I might as well finish it and try to make back some of my money.

As I'm working, my mind relaxes, and it finally clicks. Both what Leo means by what he said, and why I'm really pissed. This isn't about Hanna telling me what to do. It's about feeling out of control. I don't want to back down and seem weak. The idea that someone is out to hurt my pack makes me feel like I'm not in control anymore, and I can't stand that.

It doesn't matter that I essentially agree with her. The idea of having someone babysit me while I work is ridiculous. No one has the kind of job where they can hang out here all day. And I don't want to inconvenience my friends.

I don't want to admit that Leo is right, though. There has to be a compromise that won't seem like I'm backing down. I don't have enough orders to hire someone, even part time or temporary. Besides, I can't exactly offer Lucas that job when it's his family that we suspect is trying to hurt us. And he's the only one I could easily work with.

Knowing I'm stuck between a rock and a hard place isn't helping me to figure out what to do here. By the time I stop working, I have all of the pieces of the table sanded and prepped for assembly. I shut everything down and clean up the shop, while Leo sits in that damned chair and never says a word.

When I'm finished, I walk over to him. "Are you ready to go home?" I ask, sighing because I fully expect him to lecture me more about how wrong I was.

"If you're done with what you needed to do," he answers. I nod, and he pulls the chair away from the door, crossing his arms as I drag the door closed and lock it.

REMY

I'm not sure how long I hold Hanna after Leo leaves. All I know is that she's upset, and I'm not good at comforting an Omega who's crying. So, I do the only thing I can. I hold her and wipe her tears. When she falls asleep in my arms, I carry her up to my room and tuck her into my bed. If Leo wants to sleep next to her, he'll have to join us tonight.

Once I know that she's settled and isn't gonna wake up the moment I step away, I head back downstairs to wait for my brothers. Leo texts that they're on the way back, and I let him know that Hanna is asleep. If they wake her up, there will be consequences.

I have no idea what kind of mood Will is coming back in, so, I'm braced for a fight. But I'll do whatever I can to avoid it, for Hanna's sake.

The door opens, and I stand up from where I'd been waiting on the couch. Leo walks in first, with Will behind him. "Hanna is asleep. So, if you want to fight, we need to take it outside," I say quietly.

My youngest brother holds up his hands in surrender. "I don't want to fight. I'm sorry for the awful things I said to you earlier. I'll apologize to Hanna in the morning." Without another word, he toes off his boots and heads upstairs. His door closes quietly, and I turn to Leo.

"What the fuck did you say to him?"

"Not much, really. I just let him work it out on his own. Well, after arguing didn't get me anywhere," Leo laughs.

"I'm just glad that he's calmed down. She was pretty upset after you guys left. She cried for a long time before she fell asleep," I admit.

Leo catches me off guard, dragging me into a hug. "You took care of her, though. I'm proud of you, big brother."

I relax into the hug for a moment, then push him away. "I couldn't make her feel better, so there's nothing to be proud of."

"You didn't run," he says simply. And he's right. I could have run away from her tears, but I won't do that again.

HANNA

I wake up in the dark, in the middle of a bed, with a large body pressed on either side of me. Inhaling their scents, the familiar citrus and amaretto tells me that I'm sandwiched between Remy and Leo. For a moment, I'm sad that Will isn't here too. Then I remember our argument last night.

Since Leo is here with me, I hope that means Will came home. I reach out along our bond. I have no idea if I can even tell where he is or how he's feeling with this, but that doesn't stop me from trying. When I find a warm spot, I mentally tug it a little. I think he's fine, and probably here, but I have to know for sure.

I wiggle my way out of the bed, somehow managing not to wake Leo or Remy. After a quick shower in Leo's bathroom, I dress quickly and head downstairs to get breakfast. It's still really early, so I'm not planning to wake Remy yet. If the bakery opens a little later today, that will be okay.

I send a text to Mandi, letting her know that she and Blake can take the day off. Remy and I will be able to handle the crowd today. It shouldn't be too busy anyway.

Her response makes me smile.

MANDI: *Are you sure? You're not gonna kill him and put him in the muffins, right?*

I don't bother to respond, because no matter what I say, she's gonna assume I'm still mad at him. I make a pot of coffee and some toast. While I'm eating, I hear footsteps, then a voice clears behind me.

"Hanna, can we talk?" Will asks quietly. I don't turn around, but nod and gesture toward the chair across from me. I don't want to fight with him this morning. I hate the disconnect between us. "I wanted to say I'm sorry about yesterday. I was a jerk. I know that you're not trying to control me."

I look up, meeting his eyes as he takes the seat I offered. "I don't want to fight about it," I admit. Even with his apology, I'm not sure he's going to understand how badly I need to keep him safe.

"We're not gonna fight. I talked to Sam last night, and he's gonna stop by when he can to check on me. When he can't, he'll send someone else. I don't like it, but after I cooled off, I understand why you're worried," he says.

"Thank you." I stare at him for a few minutes, trying to figure out why it still feels off between us. Everything takes effort, and I guess we just need a little time.

Before he can say anything else, Remy and Leo come down the stairs and join us. Leo presses a kiss to my temple as he walks over to get coffee. "Are you ready? I think we're a little late this morning," Remy says, grabbing our jackets.

"We'll open a bit later than usual, but it'll be okay," I answer, shrugging into my jacket. I turn to clear the table from my breakfast, but Will has already taken care of it. Remy ushers me out the door and a few minutes later, we're working together to do prep and open the bakery.

I'm surprised at how helpful and easygoing Remy is in my kitchen. Until today, it had felt wrong to have him here. Now, it feels like this is where he belongs. We work pretty well together, mostly in the quiet of the early morning, only talking when one of us has a question. It's strange how peaceful it is.

Before my heat, I had been working on new recipes. That seems silly now, so I push those thoughts aside. Of course, Remy finds my notebook and asks about it. "What's this?" He holds up the spiral bound book. "It looks like new recipes. Are we making any of these today?"

He flips through, nodding at some pages and wrinkling his nose at others. "That's just something I was working on before. It's not important."

Remy levels me with a stare. "Don't lie to me, cupcake. This book is important to you, and I'd be happy to work on any of these with you." The earnest tone he uses makes my heart warm. It reminds me of why I fell for him in the first place.

"Okay, if you insist. Pick one and we'll try it as a special today," I offer as a compromise. I know him well enough to understand that he won't let it go, no matter how much I want him to.

"This caramel mocha coffee cake sounds good. What if we turn it into muffins or cupcakes, though?" His eyes light up with the suggestion, and I can't refuse.

"That sounds great. Why not both? Muffins for breakfast, cupcakes this afternoon? And we won't overlap, so if people want to try it, they'll have to come in twice," I suggest.

The smile that lights up his face is contagious and I find myself grinning back. "I love it. I'll get stuff together for it." Our morning continues in relative peace, and before I know it, we're ready to open.

A line at the door when Remy unlocks it shocks me. Then it starts to make sense when they all file in. With The Diner gone, there aren't many options for breakfast in town. Echo Falls is pretty small, and it seems like no one wants to cook breakfast.

Remy and I take turns working the counter and rushing back to the kitchen to bake more. "I'm sorry I gave Mandi and Blake the day off. It's crazy in here today," I say as I pass Remy to head out front.

He reaches out and drags me into his arms, pressing a hard kiss to my lips. "No apologies. I like that it's just the two of us here today. It gives us a chance to see how this might work."

I melt into him with those words. I finally feel like things are starting to come together again; like my happy ending might be just around the corner. I don't get to enjoy his embrace as long as I'd like, because there are hungry people in town, and it seems like most of them are in my bakery right now.

With a laugh, I shuffle into the kitchen to deal with the next round of baked goods while Remy waits on the line of customers. I'm thoroughly enjoying having Remy here with me, and I think he's having a good time too, even if we're slammed.

By the time our lunch rush, which is a new thing for me, is over, we're both exhausted. Remy locks the door behind the last customer, and I survey the dining room. The pastry case is empty, and the dining area is in desperate need of cleaning.

"I can't believe we sold everything," I say with a laugh.

"I think we should close early today. It's gonna take a while to clean up, and I'm pretty sure we've waited on everyone in town at least twice already," he suggests. I nod, grabbing a bottle of cleaner and a rag from behind the counter.

Remy and I work together to clean up the dining room, the counter, then the kitchen. Once the entire bakery is spotless, he leads me out to his SUV and we go home. Home. That word seemed so strange two weeks ago, when I didn't have one. Now, I can't imagine being anywhere but with my pack.

"You can shower when we get home, and I'll get something ready for dinner. I'll send a text in the group chat to see when the guys will be home. If they're gonna be late, they can fend for themselves," Remy teases. I know he would never do that to his brothers. Even when he's mad, he cooks for his family. It's his love language.

"I'll send the text now, since you're driving," I offer, pulling out my phone. I open our group text thread and start typing.

ME: *What time will you two be home? Remy is gonna make dinner. He needs to know how much to cook and when to have it ready.*

I don't expect to get a response right away from either of them, so when my phone buzzes in my hand, it startles me. Remy laughs when I jump.

WILL: *I'll be home in a couple of hours.*

He must be having a slow day, or maybe he's taking a break. Usually, it takes him longer to respond.

I'm not worried that Leo hasn't answered yet. He's at the firehouse today, and I know that Jasper is with him. And he'll head from there to the bar to open before Simon takes over for the night. So, it might be a couple of hours before he gets back with me.

LEO

Sirens blare as Jasper and I race down County Road 462. We got a report of Miller's barn being on fire, and we were the closest. A few of the other guys are supposed to meet us out here, which is good. Jas and I can handle the truck on our own, but as big as this barn is, extra hands and hoses will make things easier.

I park the truck between the barn and the pond, since we may need to tap into an additional water source to get this blaze out. "How long has this been going?" I ask.

Jas looks at me. "I don't know. Dispatch just said they got an anonymous call." It looks like the entire barn is engulfed, and the house is at risk. We have to stop this before someone gets hurt.

We climb out of the truck, fastening our jackets and getting our helmets in place. Just like we've done a thousand other times, Jas and I get the hose hooked up and start by wetting down the house. Hopefully that will prevent the fire from spreading.

I get on the radio, calling for an additional truck and more hands. Dispatch responds that truck fifty-two is on its way, but that the other back up we'd been expecting has been delayed. A wreck on Highway 10 has them tied up. We're on our own until the guys on truck fifty-two arrive.

"It's okay, we can handle it," Jasper insists. He's the most positive person I've ever met; possibly the most stubborn, too. Next to Remy, that is. No one can truly compete with my oldest brother on stubbornness.

"I hope so," I answer. I can't help wondering if Hanna is okay. I know she worries about me when I'm fighting fires, but with the additional concern that Sheridan or someone else is trying to hurt us, I'm sure she's beside herself. Of course, that's if she even knows about this. Hopefully word hasn't spread yet. It's not like I can stop to check my phone right now.

sixteen

Wait and See

WILL

Things are off between Hanna and me today, even after I apologized. I should have expected that, but somehow, I thought she'd instantly forgive me and we'd be fine. So, when she texts to ask when I'll be home, I cut my day short. If not for her message, I probably would have stayed five or six more hours instead of the two I promised her.

Hopefully, she'll see that I'm trying. Getting angry about her wanting all of us to stay safe was childish, and I know it. I slide my phone back in my pocket and start working again, determined to finish this table before I leave.

I'm caught off guard when the door slams open. Turning to see who's here, I laugh when Lucas walks through the door. I guess I'm more nervous about the looming danger than I thought.

"What's up, Lucas?" I ask when he stalks inside. I'm barely able to put my tools down before he fists his hand in my shirt, drawing back his other to strike.

"Is your family seriously trying to pin these fires on mine?" he snarls.

"Let go of my shirt, and we can talk about this," I insist, trying to keep a level head. There are too many weapons in here for any fight to end well. I don't think he wants to hurt me, but I can't know that for sure.

"Oh, so now you wanna talk? After you went to the cops saying that we started those fires? That's convenient, isn't it?" His hand tightens on my shirt, and I'm pretty sure he's barely holding on to his control.

"Lucas, man, we've always been friends. I never said that I thought you did those fires. Your grandpa threatened my brother, and people heard him do it. That's why the cops are looking at your family. So, if you have a problem with anyone, it should be him; not us," I insist, dropping my hand to his wrist between us. Even with my short temper, I have no desire to fight with my friend. There's no evidence that he's had any part in the mess we've been dealing with, and I won't take my annoyance out on him.

I'm ready to block if he throws a punch, but I hope it doesn't come to that. He growls in frustration before releasing my shirt and backing away from me. "I know that we're friends. That's why it pissed me off so bad to think you'd accuse me and mine of something like this," he says quietly.

"I understand, man. I do. But Remy didn't even tell us about the threat until after the fire. After some of the people who'd been in The Diner and heard what your grandpa said to him had already told the cops about it. Yeah, I called Sam to talk about it, but before I could say anything about the threats, he was asking what I knew about them," I explain. "And honestly, no one thinks it was you."

"But my family," he says. "You think they did it." His anger gives way to despair, and I worry that he's gonna attack me again.

"I don't know what to think, Lucas. All I know is that Hanna was put in danger, and one of our family's businesses was destroyed. Add to that the threats your grandpa made, and what would you think?" I ask. "Especially when people are saying he made it sound like he had something to do with Hanna's fire."

A knock on the open door catches our attention. We turn to find Sam standing in the doorway, surveying the situation. I nod at him, and he walks inside. "Everything okay here, fellas?" he asks, eyeing Lucas' red face and balled up fists.

"We're just talking it out, Sam," I say, turning to Lucas. "Right?"

He nods, taking a deep breath in an attempt to calm himself. "Right."

"Well, how about we talk it out after you put the weapons on the workbench over here and step over there?" Sam asks, gesturing to Lucas.

My eyes go wide when he pulls the hunting knife from the back of his pants and does as Sam requested. I nearly choke when Lucas follows it with the gun he'd had tucked in his waistband. I'd missed that, too.

Shit. I'm gonna owe Sam a round at Leo's after this. He might have just saved my life. "Now, have a seat, Lucas. Then you can tell me why you felt like you needed to bring these weapons to a talk with your friend," Sam orders.

Without hesitation, Lucas grabs one of my camp chairs and drops into it, across the room from the bench where he just placed his weapons. "What the fuck, man?" I ask, shocked that he'd felt the need to be armed to come talk to me.

"I wasn't thinking," he insists. "I saw red when I heard the accusations. People were saying that you'd accused me of this. I know I shouldn't have believed them, but I did. I'm sorry. If you have to arrest me, Sam, I understand." He props his elbows on his knees, dropping his head in his hands.

Sam and I exchange a look. He runs a hand through his dark, messy hair. "The way I see it, you didn't hurt anyone. I'm gonna confiscate your weapons—you won't be getting those back. And I'm gonna check to make sure they haven't been used in a crime. Other than that, if Will says y'all were just talking, there's nothing wrong with that."

I give Sam a nod of thanks and turn my attention back to Lucas. "I'm sorry that the rumors got exaggerated and that you believed them. I never thought you were involved in the fires. I'm not even sure if your grandpa is. But he did threaten my family, and people heard what he said. It doesn't surprise me that they took the story and ran with it."

"I can't prove that none of them were involved," Lucas says, shaking his head. "I want to, because they're blood. But the truth is, I don't know if one of them could have done this."

"Listen, Lucas. We all want to think the best about our families. And it's good that you're not jumping to conclusions. Let me finish my investigation, and we'll get to the bottom of this, I promise," Sam insists.

LEO

"When is that truck getting here?" I ask with a cough, flipping my visor up.

Jasper looks at me and shrugs. "They should have been here by now. I'll call dispatch and see what the issue is. Can you hold this off?"

I nod and he backs away. I slap the visor back down and refocus on the fire that's trying to spread. The house is as protected as we can make it, but the woods surrounding the back of the barn are still in danger. We only have so much hose, and it won't reach where I need it.

I try to adjust my angle and spray over the barn, but that seems to push the fire in that direction. "Fuck," I breathe. Then I hear it. The most glorious sound I've ever heard. Sirens in the distance, but getting closer. After a decade with the volunteer fire department, I know that I'm hearing three distinct vehicles. One is a firetruck —probably fifty-two— one is an ambulance, and the third is a police cruiser. Back up has arrived!

As they park, Jasper comes back and takes the hose from me. I meet Jason Conley at the second truck. After filling him in on what we've done, he moves the truck to get a better angle on the woods. I finally feel like I can breathe again when something slams into the back of my head.

Falling to my knees, I turn to see what happened, but I'm seeing stars. The world blurs as I lose consciousness.

HANNA

"Will should have been home by now," I insist. "I have a bad feeling; something happened."

Remy looks at me, then nods and pulls out his phone. Before he can dial Will's number, the back door opens, and the source of my concern walks in.

"Sorry, I know I'm late. There was an issue, but Sam showed up just in time. I'm fine," Will says, crossing the kitchen to pull me into his arms. He presses a gentle kiss to my temple and I relax into him.

"What happened?" Remy asks.

Will recounts the details of Lucas showing up and attacking him over the rumors he'd heard. Oh, shit. If Lucas got that upset, what will the other Sheridan boys do when they hear those same rumors?

Remy and I exchange a look. *Leo.* My mind practically screams it, and when my Alpha nods, I know that he's thinking the same thing.

"What did I miss?" Will asks, noticing our unspoken communication.

"Leo might be in trouble. I'll call the fire house and see where he is," Remy says, pulling out his phone and walking into the living room.

"What makes him think Leo is in trouble?"

"He never answered the text earlier. I haven't heard from him all day. Yeah, I know he could just be busy, but it's not like him to ignore messages," I answer, wringing my hands together. This must be what the bad feeling was about. "And if you were attacked by one of the Sheridans because they heard the rumors, I have to wonder if the same has happened to h im."

Will wraps his arms around me again, holding me tightly. "Remy will find out where he is, then we'll go check on him. It's gonna be okay. He's fine; I'm sure of it."

I wish that his quiet reassurance was enough. I fight against the tears filling my eyes, trying to push away the thoughts of Leo being hurt or worse. And we're still not even sure it's Sheridan who's after us. It could be someone we never even considered. That thought terrifies me.

Remy walks back into the room. "Miller's barn on 462. Let's go. Dispatch said that no one has eyes on him. The fire is gaining momentum, though, so she wasn't surprised. There are only two trucks on scene."

We pile into Remy's SUV and he races toward County Road 462. I can feel along the bond that he and Will are as anxious as I am. Leo has to be okay. I can't seem to reach him through the bond, and it scares me. I don't know what we'll do if he's hurt, or, no, I can't let myself think that way. I thread my fingers together, clasping tightly and say a prayer that we're not too la te.

REMY

As much as I know that kicking myself isn't gonna help right now, I can't stop the thoughts that fly through my head as my

SUV speeds toward the fire where I hope to find my brother. This isn't my fault. But if I had stayed, I would have been there with Leo when that call came. I would have joined the firehouse when he did. We would be fighting that fire together. And we probably wouldn't have Hanna.

It's a trade off, and I have to let go of the guilt that's crushing my heart. All I can focus on right now is getting to my brother. If I pause long enough to blame myself for whatever has happened, we won't get there in time to save him.

Because somehow, I know—I just know—that Leo is in danger. Alpha sense, big brother sense, I have no idea. But I know it just as clearly as I know Hanna is ours. I park the SUV behind one of the fire trucks.

"Huh, that's weird. Dispatch didn't say anything about police being here," I say as we climb out, gesturing to the cruiser parked nearby. "Stay together. I have a feeling something is off here."

For once, no one argues with me. Hanna stays behind me, and Will protects her back. We won't be able to get close enough to the second truck without fire gear. Luckily, the guys have their names on the backs of their jackets. I don't see Kerrisk anywhere, but I do see Conley and Watson, along with a couple of others I don't know.

"Where is he?" Hanna asks, noticing the same thing I just did.

"He has to be around here somewhere," Will says, turning in a circle. "Wait. Rem, look at this. Someone else was here. Tracks." He points to the tire tracks a foot away from us.

"Can you tell what kind of vehicle?" I don't know why I expect him to know, but I do.

Will shakes his head. "No, it's too dark out here already. But let's flag down the officer over there and ask him who was with them. He might know where Leo is, too."

Hanna and I follow Will over to where the police officer is leaning into his car, talking on the radio. Once we're close enough, I recognize him as Dan Smith. He's a good guy, and I'm sure he'll help us if he can.

"Hey, Dan. Have you seen Leo?" Will asks.

"He was here when we pulled up. Huh, that's weird. Where did the ambulance go?" He looks around as if there's someone else here. "I wonder if he got hurt or something."

"Which ambulance was it?" I ask, my eyes wide, and arms wrapping around Hanna when she gasps.

"One of the older ones. I didn't recognize the EMT in it. Seemed weird that they were alone, though. Before I could check it out, I got a call from the Sheriff on the radio. You guys walked up when I finished," he explains.

Fuck. Someone in an older ambulance may have Leo. That's not much to go on. "Did you get a rig number? Or the plates?" Will asks. I'm glad he's here, because I wouldn't have had the focus to ask those questions.

Dan shakes his head. "Sorry, I didn't pay much attention."

"Was it one of the white rigs or one of the blue ones?" Hanna asks, as if something just occurred to her.

"Blue. I remember thinking it was weird that they were using one of the oldest ones, but figured the new one broke down," Dan says.

"Thanks," I say, turning to take one more look around for my brother before we start searching for this rogue ambulance.

HANNA

"He's not here. Now what do we do?" I ask. My heart races, and I can't catch my breath. Somehow, I'm certain that it has nothing to do with the raging flames a few yards away from us.

"We have to track the ambulance," Remy insists.

"But how?" I ask. Fighting against the overwhelming sense of despair, I try to focus on positive things. My bond with Leo still exists, so I know that he's alive. I don't know enough about bonding to understand if I'll be able to tell if he gets hurt, though.

"The tracks head this way. All we can do is follow them and see if we get lucky. Should we call Sam?" Will suggests.

When Remy nods in agreement, Will pulls out his phone and dials. Remy ushers me into the SUV while Will explains to Sam what we suspect. It's not a lot for him to go on, but Sam is a good detective. I hope he can come up with a way to find Leo before it's too late.

Will climbs in the back seat as he puts his phone away. "Sam is on his way. I told him which direction we were headed and what we're driving. He'll find us up the road."

"He didn't try to talk you out of going after them?" Remy asks.

"I told him not to bother. Leo is family, and we're not abandoning him to whoever wants to hurt our family. If that's Sheridan, then so be it. Or if it's someone else, we're about to find out. Either way, we're gonna take care of it," Will says.

Remy follows the tracks, slower than I expect. As badly as I want to rush, I know it won't do any good. We'll never find Leo if we lose the trail, and these tire tracks are the only thing we have to go on. I'm not sure if it's lucky or not that this road is mostly gravel and mud.

LEO

The first thing I notice is the darkness. The second is that I can't move. I wiggle my fingers and toes, testing. Okay, good. I'm not paralyzed, so I must be strapped down somehow. But why? The question echoes in my head as I try to piece together what happened.

Last I remember, I was fighting the fire at Miller's barn with Jasper. Shit, Jasper! Is he okay? Did they take him out too? Fighting the restraints, I try to keep quiet. I have no idea who is holding me or how dangerous they are. I don't want to draw unwanted attention to myself if there's a chance I can break free.

I twist my wrists, ignoring the pain as I rub them raw against the straps holding me in place. Am I strapped to a gurney? The ambulance! I knew there was something off about that. Echo Falls hasn't used the blue rigs in years.

But who was driving? My head spins when I raise it and look around. I can't tell where I am because it's so dark in here. I hear metal scraping against metal and realize that I must still be inside the ambulance. Someone is opening the doors. I lay back and close my eyes, pretending to be asleep.

I have to figure out who did this and what they want. Then I need an escape plan. How am I gonna get out of this one? Just breathe. Let's take this one step at a time. Figure out who took me, why, then worry about getting away.

"I told you he was knocked out. I don't know why you think I couldn't handle this," a feminine voice says. It's familiar, but I can't quite place it. I don't dare open my eyes, though, or I'll lose the element of surprise.

"I still don't know how you managed to get him in the rig by yourself and get out of there without anyone noticing," Bo Sheridan says. That fucker. Well, I guess that means Sheridan was behind the fires in one way or another. But which Sheridan is in charge? I guess I'll have to wait and see.

seventeen

A Brilliant Compromise

LEO

"I'M STRONGER THAN I look, Bo. You should know that by now," the woman argues. Why does she sound so familiar?

"You sure he's alive? He's not moving. Shouldn't he be awake by now?" Bo asks.

"I don't know. I hit him pretty hard. I'll check him out and make sure he's okay," she says and I hear footsteps coming closer. So much for pretending to be knocked out.

I groan and shake my head slowly as if I'm just coming to. I blink a few times at the light streaming in from the back of the ambulance.

"I bet he has a concussion. He probably won't remember any of this," she says, shining a light in my eyes.

"I'd guarantee that, since he's not gonna live through the night," Bo says with a laugh.

Schooling my expression the best I can, I stare at the blonde woman who is standing over me with a pen light. Where do I know her from? Then it hits me—she's one of them. Katie Sheridan. That's why her voice was so familiar.

"You didn't say anything about killing him. Gramps said you needed to talk to him; scare him a little," she says.

Bo laughs again, a terrifyingly cold sound. "Yeah, he knew you wouldn't help if he told you his plan."

"I'm not gonna help you hurt anyone, Bo. It's not right. Gramps said this guy was chasing after your girl, making her uncomfortable. That he and his brothers had been hiding from you when you tried to straighten things out. None of that is true, is it?" The hurt in her voice seeps into me.

"Shut the fuck up, Katie," Bo growls, slapping her across the face, then shoves her. She slams into the wall of the rig, crumpling to the floor. "Bitch talks too fucking much, ya know?" He turns his attention to me. I pretend that I don't understand what's happening here. It's my only chance of survival.

"What—what happened?" I mutter, feigning confusion. If I can convince Bo that I have a concussion, maybe I'll have a shot at getting away. "Room is spinning." It's not a complete lie, given the throbbing in my head, I'm certain I have a concussion. But I'm awake and aware enough to fight for my life. I won't let Hanna down by giving up. I need to find a way to get my hands free.

"You hit your head, buddy. It's okay. We're gonna take care of you," he says. I cringe internally at the syrupy tone he uses. Since I'm not supposed to know he plans to kill me, I don't let myself react, fighting against my body's desire to growl, buck, and throw myself at this monster.

"Why am I tied down?" I ask the question slowly, making sure to slur the words a little.

"We were worried you might fall off the gurney. I can sit you up a little, but let's not take any chances, okay?" I wonder how many times I've interacted with this Alpha and not known what he was planning against my family. He's a pretty good actor, and if I hadn't heard him say I wasn't gonna live, I might think that his family wasn't involved at all.

When he raises the head of the gurney, I can see Katie crumpled on the floor. "Is she okay? What happened to her?" As if I didn't hear the slap or the way she slammed into the wall of the rig; but two can play at deception.

"Oh, she ran into the wall. She's fine," he insists, stepping in front of me and blocking her body from view. I can't tell if she's breathing or not, but clearly Bo isn't concerned.

HANNA

Panic grips my chest, my heart beating faster than it ever has, as Remy flies down the gravel road. I have no idea how he's following the ambulance tracks, but every time I think he must have lost them, he makes a sudden turn. When he slows down to a crawl, I realize that I'm struggling to breathe. Going fast was scary, but at least it felt like we were getting somewhere. Now, it's like we're stopped. Almost like we're giving up. It's jarring how he went from driving slow to speeding to creeping ag ain.

"We have to find him," I say, not bothering to fight the tears streaming down my cheeks. To say I'm scared would be an understatement. I'm terrified that I'll never see Leo again. My sweet Beta; I can't stand the thought of losing him. He's been my constant for the past ten years, more than anyone besides my girls.

"We're gonna find him," Remy insists, threading his fingers through mine. He pulls my hand up to his lips and presses a kiss against the back of my hand.

"Rem, what's that?" Will points down a path that can't be wide enough for the SUV to go down.

"What is it?" I ask, trying to figure out what he sees.

"Blue paint on those trees. They took the rig through there. That has to be where they went. There's no sign of tracks ahead," he says.

Remy must see the paint, because he turns toward the path. "We're not gonna fit down there in this. We'll have to go on foot." He looks at me. "I would ask you to stay here, but I know you won't. So, I'll ask that you stay close to me or Will. I trust you to fight if you have to."

His words mean more to me than he realizes, and more tears fall. I'd expected him to insist that I stay in the SUV. I'd been planning to fight him on it. Hearing that Remy trusts me to fight if I need to is exactly what I need to hear. I wipe my eyes and climb out of the SUV with my Alphas. "I'll stay between you two as much as I can. And you're right, I'll definitely fight, especially if it'll help save one of you."

Remy locks the SUV, then hands me the keys. I tuck them in my pocket, understanding that he wants to make sure I can get away if something goes wrong. "Phones on silent," he orders, and we don't argue. The three of us move quietly through the trees, staying beside the path instead of going right on it. The ground is slick and muddy, but we trudge through it anyway.

The further down this path we go, the more I feel like we're not prepared for what's about to happen. I trust my guys, but I have no idea what we're gonna do if we find whoever took Leo. This feels like a horrible idea.

Will catches me when I slip in the mud again, pressing me against his chest and carrying me until the ground is a little more solid. When Remy stops short in front of us, I barely stop myself from slamming into his back. I lean around him to see what stopped him.

Right in front of us, with the back doors thrown open, is the dark blue ambulance that was reported to be on the scene at Miller's barn fire. And strapped to a gurney in the back is Leo. He doesn't look hurt, but until we can get in there, we can't tell.

REMY

The minute I see the rig, I stop. We're close enough to it that I can see Leo, and from the flicker of awareness that crosses his face, he can see me, too. I can't tell how many people we're gonna have to fight, but that doesn't matter right now. As long as Hanna can get away if things go bad, we'll be fine. Will and I can unleash our Alpha natures on these bastards and save our brother.

I turn to Hanna. "I want you to hang back and keep an eye on him while Will and I sneak around to the front of the rig. If anything goes wrong, run. Get out of here and call the Sheriff. Got it?"

When she nods in response, I press a kiss to her lips. My heart is racing, and I'm not sure I can do this. I don't have a choice. My not-so-little brother needs me. Will follows me around the passenger side of the ambulance along the tree line. I freeze when I hear voices inside. Turning to Will, he mouths, "Leo" and I nod. I can't tell who the other voice belongs to, though.

Now that we're faced with our brother's kidnapper, I wish we'd thought to bring weapons. Hopefully, Will and I are enough to get Leo out of here. We stay there, listening for a few minutes. Will and I lock eyes, both raising a single finger when we realize that Leo is alone in the rig with one man. Surely, we can take out one guy. I nod, and Will heads toward the back of the ambulance.

I follow, stopping next to the rear tire while my youngest brother peeks around the door to see who we're dealing with. He ducks back and whispers, "Bo." Fucking Bo Sheridan. Well, at least we were right about who was after us. I still don't understand why that old man has a problem with my family. What possesses someone to send their grandchildren out to hurt another pack?

An idea hits me, and I wonder if it's crazy. I motion to Hanna, hoping that she understands what I need her to do. She nods, then a moment later, she's screaming as if she's being chased. Bo jumps out of the rig, clearly panicked.

"What the fuck?" he mutters when he sees Hanna. Will and I jump him while he's distracted, knocking him to the ground. Hanna climbs into the ambulance, freeing Leo.

"Katie is in here, too. Looks like she's knocked out," Hanna calls.

"Is Leo okay?" I call back. "Can we put this asshole on the gurney and tie him down?"

"That sounds like a plan," Leo answers, helping Hanna down from the back of the rig. When Will and I drag Bo to his feet, Leo takes a swing at him. "That's for slamming Katie into the wall the way you did. Only an asshole would treat a lady that way."

Once Bo is strapped to the gurney, Will checks Katie's pulse. "She's alive, but out cold." With the threat neutralized, we climb out of the ambulance.

"I called the Sheriff. He's got guys on their way now," Hanna says when we walk up to where she and Leo are standing away from the rig. The way she's holding onto him, I can tell how scared she was. And I don't blame her. I was too.

WILL

Keeping her arms wrapped around Leo, Hanna manages to dig the keys out of her pocket and hand them to me just as the police arrive. After we answer some questions, the officers let us go. It's not like they won't be able to find us if they have more questions. Remy leads us back to his SUV, and I climb behind the wheel. Leo settles in the back seat with Hanna, and Rem gets in the passenger seat.

"This feels like the longest day ever," Hanna breathes, settling against Leo's side. He wraps his arms around her, and we head home.

"Do we need to stop by the hospital?" I ask, meeting Leo's gaze in the mirror.

He shakes his head. "I'm okay. Just need to rest."

I glance at Remy, and he nods. "We can take him later if we notice any problems. I don't think she's gonna let him out of her sight for a while." He gestures to the back seat, where Hanna is practically in Leo's lap. It looks like she's fallen asleep. Poor thing is probably drained from the adrenaline rush.

"Okay. Home it is, then," I answer, gunning it as much as I dare with Hanna sleeping. I don't want to scare her. She's been through enough today.

My concerns don't seem to matter once we arrive home. Sam is waiting for us on the front step. From the way his brows are drawn together, it doesn't look like he has good news. What else could go wrong today?

Remy takes Hanna from Leo, guiding them both into the house. "Sam," he says. "I'm gonna get these two settled, then we can talk."

Sam nods then follows us inside. Something about him being here, waiting for us, makes me nervous. He doesn't speak until Remy comes back into the living room. I offer him a drink, but he refuses.

"What's the problem?" Remy asks, calm and direct.

"Bo's gonna press charges. And I need to get a more in-depth statement from Leo. If Katie doesn't make it, he might be looking at charges too," he says with a shake of his head.

"What the actual fuck?" I ask my best friend. How could he do this to us?

"Listen, it's not that I think you guys did anything wrong. I'm convinced that Sheridan is the problem here. But this altercation comes down to one side versus the other. There were no neutral witnesses. There's no way for me to prove what actually happened."

Sam pauses, then continues, "That works out better for you guys. You'll get charged for assault, sure, but Leo can press charges for kidnapping or unlawful detainment. It'll be their word against yours, and I'm sure it'll all get thrown out. I know that's not what you want to hear."

"Not even close. That fucker took our brother and was gonna kill him. Leo says he's the one who knocked Katie out. And he's just gonna get away with it?" I growl.

Remy puts a hand on my shoulder. "Take a breath, Will. I'll handle this."

"There's nothing to handle. I'm here to arrest the three of you and take you in. I don't have a choice. Please don't fight me; I'd rather not have to call for backup," Sam says, bowing his head.

Fuck me. We're going to jail for the night, and Hanna will be here alone. This is probably just what Sheridan wanted to happen. I bet he's excited about how this is turning out.

Remy and I exchange a look. I shake my head. He nods, and turns to Sam. "I wouldn't normally do this, but Hanna was with us the whole time. If you have to arrest us, then you probably need to take her in too. Conspiracy or something."

"What the fuck are you doing, Rem? You're supposed to protect the pack, not offer us up for jail time," I whisper at him.

He glares at me. "Trust me, little brother. I know what I'm doing." He turns back to Sam, raising his eyebrows in question.

"I hadn't considered that. You're right. It's probably a good idea to take her in too," Sam agrees. "As long as you all come quietly, we don't even need cuffs."

Remy nods. "Will you let me go upstairs and get them? I give you my word, my pack will cooperate. There's no need for backup or cuffs. I'll even follow you back to the station in my car, since your cruiser is smaller than my SUV."

Sam nods. "I'll take you at your word, Remy. Do what you need to do, and I'll be down here waiting when you're ready. Just don't take all night."

My Alpha nods again, then takes the stairs two at a time, leaving me down here with my best friend. "Why would he do that?" I ask, still confused about Remy's motivations.

Sam laughs. "Because he's smarter than Sheridan. Or us."

"What do you mean?"

"If I take Hanna in with you guys, you'll be put in Pack Holding instead of the general cells. The four of you will get to stay together, and you'll know for sure that she's okay. Honestly, I wish I'd thought of it. The way Bo insisted that Hanna wasn't involved seemed off to me, but I couldn't work my head around how to not bring you guys in. This is a brilliant compromise," he explains.

My anger dissipates a bit. "So, you don't think we actually did anything wrong?" For some reason, I need his reassurance on this.

"Not even a little. But I volunteered to pick you guys up. Because Conley was gonna send someone else, and they were already talking about backup and multiple cars. I knew I could convince you guys to come in on your own. Told him that much. He respects me enough to give me this chance. Once you guys are in custody, we'll start working to get you out," he says.

Knowing that he believes me and my family makes a world of difference. "Will it all get strung together? The fires, the threats, Lucas attacking me, Katie and Bo kidnapping Leo?"

"If we can prove they were behind all of it, yeah. Right now, Bo is saying that Leo kidnapped Katie. I shouldn't tell you any of this, but I will. You need to explain this to them so they can figure out how to handle it. Bo insists that Leo took Katie, and he came upon the rig when she was about to be taken advantage of."

"Are you fucking kidding me? That asshole actually accused my bonded brother of attempted rape? That's ridiculous," I argue.

"Wait, did you say bonded? As in, you've already claimed Hanna? That could make all the difference here. I don't think everyone knows about that yet."

"It's none of their business, so they shouldn't," I insist.

"But you may have to go public with when it happened to prove that Bo is lying," Sam argues.

"It's not like bonding records are hidden. I had to file more paperwork after Hanna's heat. If someone wanted to know, they could find out," Remy says. I didn't realize he'd come back downstairs.

EIGHTEEN

Uncomfortable

HANNA

I HAVE TO ADMIT, I was not expecting for Remy to wake me up and tell me to get dressed. When I ask what's going on, he briefly explains that we're going to jail. To jail. As prisoners. As in we're being arrested. What?!

"What the actual fuck?" I ask him, my eyes wide.

"It's fine. I promise, I have it handled. Yes, we're gonna get arrested and processed. It'll be okay. Because Sam is arresting the whole pack, they have to keep us together. I'm sorry, cupcake, but it was the only way to keep you safe," Remy says, shoving his hoodie at me.

I take a minute to process his words, unsure how to feel about the situation. As much as I want to stay with them, I don't want to go to jail. I'm not sure how going to jail will keep me safer than me staying here.

I pull his sweatshirt on over my tank and leggings. I want to argue with Remy more, but my Beta sighs, catching my attention. Turning to look at Leo, I can't help asking, "Are you okay?"

He nods. "Not thrilled about the situation, but at least we get to stay together." His words take every bit of fight out of me. Even if arguing would keep me out of jail, I don't want to be away from my pack.

Once we're downstairs, we overhear part of Will's conversation with Sam. It hadn't occurred to me that people didn't know we were bonded. I wasn't keeping it a secret like Will seemed to think.

When Remy admits as much, Will jumps. He didn't see us come down the stairs because he was busy defending my right to privacy. It's sweet but unnecessary.

"Remy's right. It's not a secret. I figured the whole town knew by now, but I guess not," I say. "Can we get this over with? I'm not looking forward to jail, but the sooner we go, the sooner we can come home."

Sam agrees, taking a minute to read us our rights and verify that we understand if we resist at this point, he'll have to call for backup and things will get worse. I think he's saying that for Will's sake, but it doesn't matter. We're going to the station. Together.

I'm surprised that Sam lets Remy drive us, following him to the station. But it is a small town, and things are done differently here sometimes. That may be an understatement.

Sam ushers us into the Sheriff's station, guiding us to his desk. There's only one chair besides his, so he offers it to me. "Leo needs to sit more than I do," I insist.

I don't argue when Leo sits, then pulls me onto his lap. It's the first real public display we've had, and it freaks me out a little. I remind myself that we're bonded, so it's acceptable behavior, and that helps. We answer questions as Sam fills out paperwork for our arrests, handling them one at a time.

When he gets to me, finally, I hand over my ID and his eyes go wide. "You got this updated quickly," he says with a chuckle.

I know he's referring to the fact that it no longer says "Hanna Evans," instead reading "Hanna Kerrisk." I didn't even bother to tell my guys that I'd updated it.

"It's required for an Omega to update their ID once they are claimed by a pack," I say clearly, probably louder than I should. I don't care if the whole station hears me. And it's clear that they do. Chatter around us stops, and several heads turn our way. "Since I am the Omega of the Kerrisk pack now, I had my ID updated. I'm simply following the law, Detective Nolan."

It probably sounds colder than I mean it to, and I hope that Sam doesn't take offense. But I'm sick of being jerked around because I'm an Omega. This town keeps trying to treat me like I don't matter, and I'm done with that. As a bonded Omega, I know that changes my social status, and as much as I don't care about that, I'm willing to use it to my advantage here.

"Would you prefer that I call you Hanna, or Mrs. Kerrisk?" he asks politely. When he winks at me, I know it's for the benefit of the others watching us.

I straighten my spine, wrapping Leo's arm around me tighter. Remy drops a hand on my shoulder. "Mrs. Kerrisk, please."

"Yes, ma'am," he answers. Once he's finished typing up the records, he leads us down a hall to get fingerprinted and our pictures taken. I have to admit, for mugshots, they don't turn out half bad. He explains that we each get one phone call, but I have no idea who to reach out to. There isn't anyone who could help us in this situation. I could call one of the girls, but there's nothing they could do, and I don't want to worry them over it.

I understand now that this is why Remy insisted that Sam arrest me too. "I'll have to put you in a Pack Holding cell. You'll stay together, unless one of you is pulled for questioning," Sam explains.

It's thoughtful of him to explain the process, since none of us has been arrested before. I have to fight back waves of laughter at how ridiculous this situation is. Leo gets kidnapped, and we end up arrested for saving his life. At least I know that Bo is in a holding cell, too.

"Have there been any updates on Katie?" I ask, desperately wanting the Beta to be okay so she can explain what she did, and that we were only defending ourselves.

Sam shakes his head. "Not yet. She seems to be stable for now. They're running tests at the Medical Clinic. I'm hoping they don't have to take her to General."

At least she's still in town; that's a good sign. General is the hospital in the next town over, an hour and a half away from Echo Falls. It's the closest hospital to us, and people only get moved there for things our clinic can't handle. Hopefully, Katie won't need that.

The metal bars clink shut with us inside the cell. I'm relieved that we get to stay together, but this room is far from comfortable. Wooden benches line the back wall, and there is an almost see-through privacy screen around the bathroom area.

WILL

As annoyed as I am at this situation, I have to admit, my heart fills with pride when Hanna insists that Sam call her Mrs. Kerrisk. I'm sure he understands her reasoning, and it should help us when we finally get proof that the Sheridans are the ones who've been trying to hurt us.

There's no privacy here, so I have no idea how we'll discuss our defense or anything related to the charges being brought against us. Especially with Bo Sheridan in the cell across from us.

We're left in the cell overnight, forced to do the best we can to get comfortable on the wooden benches while Bo randomly growls things at us. The only reason I keep my temper in check is that Hanna sleeps against me. Otherwise, I'd be trying to fit through the bars to get to him.

My mind races as time passes slowly. I know my brothers and I are focused on keeping Hanna as comfortable as possible. It doesn't matter that this bench is hard and cold against my back. Our Omega is stretched out on top of me, sleeping as peacefully as possible for now.

A couple of hours later, she shifts. "I can move so you'll be more comfortable," she offers, pushing up from my chest. I try to argue, but Remy holds out a hand to her. Before I can voice my desire for her to stay curled up on me, she moves to use him as her pillow. I can't blame her for needing everyone in her pack. I know it's not a slight against me.

A few hours later, I hear Hanna moving again. I look over to find her snuggled up with Leo, checking on his injuries before burying her face in his chest. By now, she'll carry all of our scents on her, and that should help her sleep better. I find myself wishing that we were back home where we could take care of her properly. When will this nightmare be over?

I squeeze my eyes shut tightly, willing my body to relax so I can get some sleep. I'm not sure how much rest we're gonna be able to get while we're locked up here. Hell, we don't even know how long we're gonna be locked up. The best plan is to be ready for anything. At least we're locked in here together. Knowing that no one can get to Hanna without going through us makes it easier to sleep, even if it's not comfortable.

It's early when Sam comes back to our cell. "You have a visitor," he says quietly as he unlocks the door. The four of us move quickly, desperate to be anywhere but here. None of us took advantage of our call last night, unsure of who to contact. I don't know anyone who could help us out of this situation. Given that, I'm curious who would have known we're here and wanted to visit us.

Sam leads us to an interrogation room and my jaw drops when I see Mayor Barry sitting in a chair, waiting for us. We're ushered inside and directed to chairs opposite the mayor. I'm not sure what to expect here. It doesn't look like the mayor is upset with us, but I don't know her well enough to know for sure what she's thinking.

Once we're seated, I can tell that Hanna is uncomfortable, so I pull her onto my lap. If we weren't bonded, it would be completely inappropriate, but since we are, no one will say a word. Except that I'm not certain that everyone knows our status yet. I can't waste time worrying about that. I'm simply comforting my Omega during a stressful situation. If someone wants to confront me about it, I'll deal with that when it happens.

REMY

Seeing Mayor Barry waiting for us eases my nerves a little. Hopefully, she'll be able to help us out of this situation. "Mayor, it's nice to see you, even under these circumstances," I say as everyone settles into their seats.

Will pulls Hanna onto his lap, and I'm glad he's holding her. That leaves me free to beg the mayor for help for my pack.

"Remy, what in the world is going on here? Sam called me about the whole situation last night after your pack refused their phone calls. You could have called me," she says.

Oh, shit. Please tell me that not wanting to bother her isn't gonna be what keeps us in jail. "I'm sorry. I should have called you. It was foolish of me to worry about appearing to ask for favoritism." She smiles at my apology. Good. There's still a chance that she'll help.

"I'll be honest, it doesn't look good. Unless Bo recants his story and confesses, or Katie comes to and tells a different story than what he's been saying, I'm not sure what I can do to help. But I wanted to at least let you know that you have my support," she says carefully.

Fuck. That's not what I wanted to hear. I understand that her hands are tied though. "So, unless or until Katie wakes up, we're stuck here?" Leo asks.

"I've got Alvin doing what he can to release you. It's not an easy situation to navigate," she explains. It's impressive if she has the Sheriff working on helping us. "We may be able to get you out on bail, but unless Bo's story is recanted or proven untrue, you'll still end up in court over this."

It's not what we want to hear, but at least she's not sugarcoating it. We need to know what we're up against so we can figure out how to deal with this. "Thank you, ma'am. We appreciate your help and your honesty," I say.

She looks at me for a moment, then turns her attention to Hanna. "I take it you've claimed your Omega?" she asks me while staring at Hanna. I hate the way people do that. Omegas are people too, and she should be directing the question to Hanna, not me. But it's politics, I guess. Showing an Alpha respect by not addressing their Omega is a weird custom, but it's not new.

"We have. And we're adjusting well, besides this situation," I answer, not missing the way my brother's arms tighten around our girl. An almost burnt syrup smell wafts on the air, and I'm not sure if Hanna is scared or pissed. An overwhelming urge to protect her surges in my chest. That's new. I've always wanted to protect Hanna; I've just never felt it hit me with this much force before.

"If you need to ask Hanna anything, you may. We can even leave the room if you think we'll influence her answers," I offer. Hanna levels a glare at me, and I feel her anger along the bond. Reaching over, I take her hand, giving it a reassuring squeeze. I try to send as much comfort as I can down the bond in response. I'm sure she'll yell at me about this later, but I'm doing what needs to be done.

"I don't want to make you uncomfortable, Hanna. However, getting your statement without the Kerrisk men in the room might be helpful," Sam says. I nod, turning to see Hanna's reaction.

Somehow, hearing that from Sam seems to have calmed her. "If that will help get us out of here, then I'll do it." She looks up at Sam, then over at Mayor Barry. "Will you both be there? Or do I have to talk to someone else?"

They exchange a look and the mayor nods. "We will be the ones interviewing you, if that's acceptable to your pack," Sam offers. I know that makes Will more comfortable, since Sam is his best friend. He's a good guy, so I know I have nothing to worry about. He won't try to influence her answers or coax her into saying anything that's not true. It also helps that I'm fairly certain he's in love with one of our girl's best friends.

I lock eyes with each of my brothers before looking at Hanna. "If that's what you want, we'll agree. If you'd rather talk to someone else, I'll insist as Pack Alpha. You tell me who you're comfortable with."

Her glare softens, and I see the moment she realizes that I wasn't being a dick. "I'll talk to Sam and the mayor," she says so quietly that I'm not sure she even spoke out loud.

LEO

We're led back to the cell, leaving Hanna in the interview room alone with Sam and Mayor Barry. "I don't like this," I whisper to Remy. I can't help locking eyes with Bo Sheridan as we walk past.

Bo yells out at us as the door to our cell closes. "Where'd your little Omega bitch go? Is she alone? Maybe I'll go see her when I get out of here today. I'll show her what a real Alpha is like."

I bristle at his words, trying to hide my reaction. Will nudges me, "Don't give him the satisfaction of reacting." For a moment, I'm amused that my hot head brother is the one who's telling me not to react. Normally, I would be the one telling him to calm the fuck down.

Something about Bo rubs me the wrong way, probably because I know he's the one who was behind my kidnapping. My head throbs, reminding me of what I went through less than twenty-four hours ago. It seems like only a few minutes and a million years at the same time. So much has happened that I'm struggling to process it all.

"I don't like leaving her alone like that. She's not safe unless she's with us," I insist, gripping Remy's arm.

"Leo, are you okay?" he asks, glancing from where my knuckles turn white at my grip back to my face. "You look kinda pale, bro."

"Let's get him on his back so he doesn't get hurt when he passes out," Will suggests, speaking to Remy instead of me. The room spins, and the room goes dark for a moment.

When I come to, I'm lying on my back on one of the cold wooden benches, staring up at the ceiling. I can hear Remy talking quietly to someone standing outside our cage, but can't quite focus enough to understand what he's saying.

I try to sit up, but Will's hand presses to my shoulder. "Just lay still, bro. It's okay. Relax." Since the room is still spinning, I don't fight him on it. Closing my eyes, I try to focus on Remy's conversation.

"You need to let Sam know that my brother needs medical help. He's got a concussion from being kidnapped yesterday. We hadn't even had a chance to get him to the hospital to be checked out before Sam picked us up," he explains.

The muttered response makes Will tense up. "What did they say?" I ask, staring at my youngest brother as he grinds his teeth.

"Apparently, he thinks Bo is telling the truth about what happened to Katie. This guy doesn't think you should get medical attention because of what you did. It doesn't matter that we know you didn't," Will says, holding up a hand to stop me from getting up. He knows that I'm itching to get my hands on not only Bo, but also the guy who is dumb enough to believe him over us.

The guy walks away, and I expect Remy to come back, but he stays next to the bars until someone comes back. They hand him something before walking away. "Here, Leo, drink this," Remy insists, pushing a bottle of water into my hand and helping me sit up.

NINETEEN

The Day That Won't End

HANNA

As SOON AS MY pack is led from the room, an uncomfortable silence fills the space. I wonder if they're waiting for me to volunteer information or if this really will be an interrogation. My Omega nature starts to take over, making me want to fold in on myself. For a moment, I regret agreeing to this. I want to be back in the cell with my pack.

Before anyone speaks, I take a deep breath. My concern for Leo outweighs my discomfort here. "Leo needs to see a medic. He has a head injury, and probably has a concussion."

Mayor Barry turns to Sam. "You didn't have him checked out before putting him in the cell?"

Sam shakes his head. "They said he was fine. I didn't realize he'd been hurt. We were busy getting Bo's broken nose taken care of."

"You need to get someone on that immediately. If something happens to him, the entire precinct will be in trouble," she insists.

Sam nods and rushes from the room, hopefully on his way to get someone to check out my mate. I give the mayor a small smile. "Thank you."

"Don't thank me yet. I understand what's happened is not what I've been told, but I'm going to have to ask you some difficult questions. I need you to promise that you'll be honest with me. I can't help you if I don't know every detail," she says.

Discomfort settles again, but I nod. "Whatever you need," I answer. It doesn't matter how uncomfortable I am, I have to protect my pack. The three of them have done everything they can to protect me, now it's my turn.

My next few minutes are spent showing the mayor my mate marks and answering questions about when they claimed me. By the time Sam returns, Mayor Barry glances at the clock. "It's clear to me that this is going to take a while. I'll have someone bring us food. There's no reason for you to suffer with jail slop, since you're cooperating. Don't worry, I'll get enough for the Kerrisk boys, too."

I thank her as she steps out to take care of breakfast. While she's gone, I fill Sam in on what she asked me and how I answered while he was gone. "Is Leo being checked out?"

"I had an officer take him to the clinic for Doc Marty to see him. As soon as they know anything, they'll let me know," he explains.

Mayor Barry comes back into the room and takes her seat. "Shall we discuss the events of last night?"

"I'm happy to tell you what I know, but I wasn't there when Leo was taken or when Katie was knocked out. So, I can't explain what happened there." I tell our story, explaining how we found the ambulance and distracted Bo to get Leo free. They ask questions to clarify my explanation, picking apart details and making sure I don't change my story. Since I'm telling the truth, I repeat every detail as many times as it takes.

A few more questions asked and answered later, the food arrives. We take a few minutes to eat before starting back again. After we've gone over everything three more times, I yawn and stretch. Sitting here is making me stiff, and I'm uneasy about Leo being away.

"I think that's enough for now," Sam says. "I'll take you back to the cell, then call and check on Leo. We should know something soon."

As we stand up to leave the room, Sam pulls out his phone. "One sec," he says, tapping the screen to answer. "Yeah." He listens for a minute, says, "Okay," then hangs up.

"Was that about Leo?" I ask, my eyes wide.

"It was. He's fine. It's a mild concussion. They're gonna keep him for observation for a few hours, then he'll be back.

Let's go tell his brothers, shall we?" Sam asks, opening the door and guiding me back to the cell where most of my pack waits for me.

REMY

Finding out that Leo is gonna be okay is a relief. My concern automatically shifts from my brother to our Omega. "Are you sure you're okay? They questioned you for a long time."

Hanna smiles at me. "It's fine. I'm good. Did they bring you breakfast?"

I nod, but Will answers before I have a chance. "Yeah, and it was awesome. They musta ordered from the bakery." I'd had the same thought, but everything was unwrapped when it got to us, so there was no packaging to inspect. I wondered how Hanna managed to get us breakfast, but I'm not sure I want to ask.

"Good. Mayor Barry insisted on getting us food. She feels bad about the situation, and is doing what she can to get us out." I can tell there's more she wants to say, but this is not a private conversation.

Waiting for Leo to return makes the rest of the day drag on. There are so many more productive things I could be doing than sitting here staring at the wall. At one point, Will starts doing pushups and crunches. I join him for a while, leaving Hanna to watch. As soon as her scent starts to permeate the area, I freeze. "Will, this is a bad idea. She's getting excited and there's nothing we can do about it right now," I mutter to my brother.

"Fuck," he swears under his breath. With nothing else to do, we move to the benches and try to get comfortable.

"Sorry. I didn't mean to mess up your workout," Hanna whispers. I smile at her, loving the way her cheeks turn pink.

"It's okay. We didn't consider the effect it would have on you. We should be the ones apologizing," I insist. "No one wants you to be uncomfortable. I hate that we had no choice but to get you arrested too."

I don't think she sees it that way, but I won't assume that she's as okay with it as I am. There was no choice; her safety is more important than having a clean record.

"I didn't understand at first, but after talking to the mayor and Sam, I think I get why you didn't think there was a choice. There was—just so you know—but I understand," she says, closing her eyes.

I think the worst part of being in jail is the boredom. At least I get to keep my pack together and ensure my Omega stays safe. I keep reminding myself of that when we run out of things we can discuss in public. We need some pack time, but can't do anything about that here.

I'm certain it's gonna take a long time to make this up to Hanna. And I will, without complaint. I'll start as soon as we're released from this cell.

LEO

I try to relax while I'm being caged in for an MRI of my head. "Are you claustrophobic?" the radiology tech asks.

"No, but I don't like not being able to move my head," I say, careful to hold very still.

"It'll be over soon. The doctor just wants to be sure he's not missing anything," she says. The process isn't as bad as anticipated, and takes less than half an hour.

"How much longer do I have to be here?" I ask when she pulls me from the machine and removes the cage holding my head still.

"I'm not sure. The doctor will get the results in about an hour. Maybe you'll be able to go home after that," she says. I'm a little surprised that she doesn't know I won't be going home. I'll be going back to jail.

The nurse is waiting to wheel me back to my room. But I'm stuck on the fact that I'll be going back to jail. Fucking Bo Sheridan. I'm still not even sure what he thought he'd accomplish by kidnapping me.

That thought reminds me that Katie is here somewhere. I doubt they'll tell me anything about her, but I can't help asking. "Is Katie Sheridan doing any better? I heard she had an accident," I say.

"I heard it wasn't an accident, but I don't know much more than that. She's got some broken ribs and a pretty bad concussion. She woke up a couple of hours ago, but I think she's resting again," the nurse explains.

"I'm glad she's doing better," I admit, keeping to myself just how much I need Katie to be well enough to explain what happened to Sam or Conley. That's the only way we're getting out of this without doing substantial jail time. I'm so pissed at the situation that I'd love nothing more than to be locked up with Bo where I could kick his ass.

I remind myself to breathe. I can't harm Bo. That would help him more than hurt. And the last thing I want to do is help that asshole. I'm anxious to get back to the jail and see Hanna. I need to make sure that she's okay. The fact that they wouldn't let me tell her goodbye when they brought me here nearly broke me. I need her as much as she needs me.

As soon as I get settled in my hospital room, Sam shows up. "Are you here to take me back?" I ask, fully expecting that I won't get to talk to the doctor before I head back to jail. Sam shakes his head.

"Not yet. Depending on how my conversation with Katie goes, you may not be going back at all. Well, not in the same capacity as you were in when you headed over here earlier, anyway," he says.

"So, she's awake and able to talk?" I don't bother to tell him that I'd asked the nurse about her, and knew that she was mostly okay.

"Yeah. They let me know while I was still questioning Hanna. They also said that you'd be having some tests, but you're expected to have a full recovery," he says. "I have to go talk to Katie, but I'll be back in a bit."

"Thanks for doing your job. Some guys wouldn't bother to try and find out the truth," I admit. He nods and disappears out the door. I'm left to wait and wonder who will make it back to me first, the doctor or Sam.

WILL

When Remy points out that exercising is getting Hanna excited, part of me wants to keep going. I'd love to see our pretty little Omega lose control. Then I realize it's not fair to her for me to push that way, especially when we have no privacy. My brother and I resort to lying down on the benches on either side of her, just out of reach. She needs time to calm down, and if I'm honest, I do too.

I always want her, but her maple cinnamon scent surrounding me nearly pushes me over the edge. I refuse to do anything that would disrespect her or make her uncomfortable, so I decide to embrace the boredom.

Now that we know Leo is gonna be okay, there's nothing to stress over. I'm sure there are more details that we'll get from our brother when he gets back. No one has updated us about Katie recently, and I'm a little concerned about that. We all want her to be okay, and not just because it's better for us if she is. Bo shouldn't have attacked her.

I'd like to get my hands on him for that alone, but I know that I can't touch him. Our situation is delicate, and I have to use restraint. I don't have to like it. I hate guys who abuse women, whether they're related to the women or not. Leo gave us the impression that Katie didn't really understand what she was doing. No doubt, Bo lied to her and convinced her that she was helping to save Hanna from us. It's the type of thing I could see him doing.

I just don't understand what he thought he'd accomplish. Did he really think that Hanna would ditch us for him if he hurt Leo? The stupidity of some people astonishes me.

The longer we sit here, the more frustrated I get. It's only one day, and I know it won't make a big difference in my orders. I'll still get everything done on time, as long as we're not stuck in here much longer. "How long do you think they'll keep us here?" I ask, turning my head to look at Remy.

"No idea. I was hoping that we'd hear something without spending too much time in jail. It's been a long week, and we'd be better off at home resting," he answers.

"Which is exactly where you're headed," Sam says. He turns to Bo. "Your cousin is awake, and told me everything. I know that you lied, and that you're the one who convinced her to help you kidnap Leo. There's no arguing that she's been influenced by them or intimidated, because none of them have seen or talked to her."

Bo's muttered curses reach us in our cell, and I barely hold back my laughter. "Are we really getting out of here?" I ask when Sam walks over.

He shakes his keys at me in response before opening the door and motioning for us to exit. I hop off the bench and help Hanna to her feet. We follow Remy out the door, pausing while Sam locks it back. Then he leads us back to the interrogation room we were in earlier.

Leo is waiting for us, with our phones, keys, and wallets. "Are you okay?" Hanna asks, throwing herself at him and hugging tightly.

"I'm good, buttercup. Just a mild concussion. I'm not allowed to drive for a couple of days. Other than that, I'm okay to do whatever I feel like," he answers. I can't help hearing the innuendo of his words, especially paired with the way Hanna blushes.

"Well, let's get this paperwork finished so you can head home," Sam says, setting papers in front of each of us. "You just need to review this page, verify that all your belongings are accounted for, and sign the last page agreeing that you understand the charges against you are being dropped."

We do as he instructs, each of us signing and handing the papers back to him. When we're finished, he leads us to the parking lot. "You know I didn't want to do this in the first place, right?" he asks as he walks us out. "I didn't have a choice. Bo claimed all kinds of crazy things, and Conley figured it would be better to bring you in to sort it out."

"We understand, Sam. You were just doing your job. A job that you're very good at, if I may say so," Remy says, shaking

Sam's hand. He sighs in relief. It seems my best friend was worried about alienating my pack.

HANNA

The four of us are exhausted. No one got much sleep while we were in jail. I still can't believe that we spent the night in jail. The situation is insane. It gets worse when Remy parks his SUV and we make it to the front door.

The living room windows are busted out. "What the hell?" Remy says, pulling out his phone. "Everybody back in the SUV. I'm calling Sam."

We pile back into the car, waiting with the doors locked until Sam arrives. This couldn't have been Bo, since he was in jail the whole time we were. Does this mean he had more accomplices? Suddenly Remy wanting me to be in jail with him makes perfect sense. I sigh in relief at the fact that I wasn't home when this happened.

Leo pulls me into his arms in the backseat, holding me close. When Sam pulls up behind us, Will and Remy get out to talk to him, leaving me in the car with my Beta. Today is the first time I've ever felt like I might not be safe with my guys. If someone is in the house, waiting for us—I can't even imagine what could have happened if we hadn't noticed the windows. Or if they'd busted out the back ones instead of the front.

"Leo, I'm scared," I admit.

"It's okay, buttercup. We'll keep you safe. Sam will find whoever did this and arrest them. We can get the windows fixed in the morning. I'm sure Will has some plywood at his shop that we can go get to cover the hole until we can get new windows. I promise, we will fix this," he says, hugging me tighter.

As scared as I am, I believe him. These men will do everything they can to protect me. They'll go out of their way to make sure I have everything I want. And right now, what I want is to feel safe in my own home.

"Do you think Remy will agree to a security system?" I ask, unable to keep the words from spilling out.

"For you? There's no way he'll argue with that. I'm sure we can get that installed in the morning, too," he assures me.

We watch as another police cruiser pulls up on the street and two more officers walk through the yard. Sam meets them at the door, the three of them drawing their guns and heading inside. "What are they doing?" I ask, my eyes wide.

Leo laughs. "They're gonna check the house and make sure no one is in it. Once they're done, Will and I can go get the plywood to cover the windows. We'll keep you safe, buttercup." I feel dumb for not realizing exactly why Remy called the police. Of course, it was to make sure the house was clear and safe for us to be inside.

"This feels like the day that won't end," I admit, closing my eyes and resting my head against Leo's chest.

TWENTY

It All Comes Out

REMY

"I UNDERSTAND THAT YOU didn't have people watching the house, Sam. I'm not saying you should have. I'm saying that I want this investigated to the best of your ability. Fingerprints, DNA, footprints, whatever physical evidence you can find to prove who did this and bring them in for it," I say.

I'm not even upset about the window so much as the added stress it puts on Hanna and Leo. She needs to rest, and he needs time to recover. I can't take care of my pack if someone is running around terrorizing them and I do nothing to stop it. Since I'm trying to avoid jail time, I have to rely on Sam to do his job.

"I understand that, Remy. And that's the only reason I'm not telling you that you need to watch how you talk to me. You know that I'll do my job and find out who did this. I will arrest them, and they will be held responsible. I suggest you get some cameras and a security system installed as soon as possible. Even with Mrs. Robinson across the street, you need more protection." He pauses, then as if he's just realized what he said, continues. "I'll go talk to her and see if she saw anything."

When he walks across the street to meet the old woman who's been watching this entire mess through her front door, I turn my attention back to Will. "You have plywood at the shop? Enough to cover the windows?"

"I do. I'll take Leo with me to get it. Don't worry, I'll make sure he's okay, and won't let him do much," he offers. I nod and he walks over to my SUV where we left Leo and Hanna to wait for the house to be cleared.

She walks over to me quickly as my brothers get into Will's truck and head over to the shop. "How do they do that?" she asks, pointing toward Will's truck as it heads away from us.

"Do what?" I ask in response.

"They came up with the same idea and didn't even discuss it. Reminds me of that trippy twin shit the Jacobs brothers used to do when we were in school," she says.

I laugh. "They've had a lot of time to get in sync with each other. Honestly, I probably had the same idea they did. Our dad taught us to work together pretty well. Sometimes we get it right," I say.

I lead Hanna inside. "Should we clean up?" she asks. I shake my head.

"Not yet. Sam's guys still have to fingerprint and investigate. Clean up will have to wait. Will and Leo won't even be able to put the plywood up until they're done. But at least we'll have it here." I take her hand and pull her toward the kitchen. She hasn't eaten since breakfast, and I'm planning to fix that.

Guiding her to a chair, I walk over to the fridge to see what I can make her. "How does grilled cheese sound?" I ask, holding up a couple of different cheeses.

"Are you gonna make it fancy?" she asks in return, a grin spreading across her face.

"I'll make it as fancy as you want it. I hope you know that I will give you whatever you want, as long as it's in my power to do so," I admit. Her cheeks blush and I grin at her. I carry cheese and bread options over to the table and help her decide which ones she wants in her sandwich. As expected, Hanna has a pretty good idea of what pairs well together, choosing sourdough with Colby and pepper jack.

I use a mixture of mustard and mayo on the bread, browning it perfectly before layering the cheese and finishing them up. By the time Leo and Will return with the plywood, I have four beautiful grilled cheese sandwiches waiting for the pack. I plate our late lunch with pickles and chips, internally annoyed that I don't have any coleslaw or salad to go with it.

Hanna doesn't seem to mind, reaching for the plate as I carry it to the table for her. My heart skips at her reaction to me taking care of her. I'm so far gone for this woman, and I wouldn't have it any other way. Now I just have to find a way to make sure she's safe.

LEO

"She doesn't want to admit it, but Hanna was terrified that someone attacked the house like that. I really think that she'd convinced herself that we were worried about her for nothing. As much as I want to keep her safe, I don't want her scared to be at the house alone if she needed to be. We need to get a security system and figure out how to make her feel better," I explain to Will.

"I'm pretty sure Sam said nearly the same thing to Remy when they were talking about the windows. We'll talk to him about it when we get back, but I'd put money on him already having a plan to get it done," Will responds.

We carry the plywood from his shop to his truck. "Do you think two pieces is enough?" I ask.

"I'm sure it'll be plenty. Hopefully the cops will be done with what they need to do so we can get it installed when we get back. But either way, at least we'll have it," he says.

Once the truck is loaded, I follow Will back to the shop to lock up. When he sets an alarm, I raise an eyebrow. "How long have you had that?"

"Years, man. Wood isn't cheap, and neither is my work. You have an alarm system on the bar, and Dad had one on The Diner. Why does mine surprise you?" he asks.

I shake my head. "I just didn't know about it."

On the way home, we talk about my hospital visit. The doctor didn't tell me much, besides that I have a mild concussion and need to take it easy for a couple of days. I admit to my brother that my head is still throbbing, and that the pain meds they gave me didn't really help. Will makes me promise to tell him if it gets worse.

WILL

The police cruiser is still in front of our house when we pull up, so I know they're not done with their investigation yet. We head inside to see how Hanna is doing, finding Remy and her at the table with lunch. "This looks delicious," I say, lunging toward a chair.

Remy laughs at me, but I don't care. I'm starving. Leo sits on the other side of Remy, and we dig in. They fill us in on what the cops have said so far, which isn't much. There are a few partial prints, but no DNA or other physical evidence yet. We may not find out who did this after all. It doesn't matter that we already know who's responsible. Knowing isn't the same as having proof.

"So, they get away with it because they got us arrested and managed not to leave prints behind. This is ridiculous," I growl, slamming my fist on the table.

"I know it's frustrating, little brother, but we have to let the police do their jobs. Sheridan will screw up—hell, he already has. Katie's statement will help put Bo away for the kidnapping and the attack on her," Remy says.

"But whichever relative did this is gonna get away with it because we don't have anything to prove it was them," I insist. The situation pisses me off more than it should. I let the anger hide my fear. I'm terrified that we won't be able to protect Hanna.

"So, we wait. We let them investigate. We stick together as much as we can, and we cooperate with the cops. We report everything Sheridan, or anyone else, says and does," Leo offers.

I don't like it, but I can't argue with his reasoning. "Fine," I agree, biting into my sandwich.

HANNA

I can feel the rage rolling off Will, and I understand it. My emotions are all over the place. I don't understand how someone who claims they wanted me for their grandsons could possibly do these things that potentially put me in danger. None of it makes sense.

I've never given Sheridan or his grandsons any indication that I might be interested in becoming their Omega. Because I have zero interest in anyone but my pack. The Kerrisk boys have always been it for me. If I can't be with them, I'll be alone. There won't be any replacement pack or second claiming. This pack is my choice.

I don't know how to make Sheridan understand that. There has to be something I can say or do to make this more clear for them. Then maybe they'll drop all this nonsense and leave us alone.

"Is there anything else we can do? I hate to admit that I'm more than a little scared of what they're gonna try next," I say, drawing my pack's attention to me.

"We're gonna protect you," Remy assures me.

"I know you will. But that doesn't stop the fear. I just want them to leave us alone. But unless we can prove it's them doing all these things, they're not gonna stop. Not until they get what they want. And we don't even know what that is anymore," I argue.

"I think they still want you. But what I don't understand is why they waited until Remy came home to start any of this," Will answers.

I shake my head, not wanting to get into this at all. I should have told them before, but didn't think it would go this far. "They didn't," I say.

"What do you mean?" Remy asks.

Leo looks at me. "I should have known. And you should have told me they were the ones harassing you."

"What are you talking about?" Will asks.

The three of them focus on me, and I try to shrink in my chair. "You can tell them, or I can. Either way, it all comes out today. And we're gonna tell Sam about it, too," Leo insists. "Now that I know who it was, we can take care of it."

I nod, knowing that he's right. I hadn't expected any of this. "I didn't think it was a big deal. Jesse Sheridan asked me out a few times, and I turned him down. Every time. That led to him kind of stalking me for a while. But then he stopped, and I thought that he'd decided to let it go."

"That's not all of it," Leo warns, and for a moment, I wish I'd never told him about the wanna be suitors that I'd rejected and their reaction.

I shake my head. "No, it's not. The stalking was scary. It started with notes and gifts that were left for me at the shop or on my porch. They were creepy, and I got rid of all of them immediately. So, I don't have proof of that, either."

"We still have to tell Sam. He can investigate and maybe someone will remember seeing something out of the ordinary," Remy says. He nods to Will, who pulls out his phone and steps away.

"I'm not happy that you kept this from us, but I understand wanting to forget it. If we had known, fuck. There's no point in blaming you for not telling us. It won't change anything. I wish you'd felt comfortable enough to tell us what was happening. I know I wasn't here, and that's my fault. But my brothers were, and you didn't tell them the whole story, either." Remy doesn't sound angry, and that's somehow worse than if he was yelling at me. I feel like I've let them down, and it feels awful.

"With you gone, it seemed pointless to get Leo and Will worked up about it. There wasn't anything they could do without getting in trouble with the Council. And it didn't last that long," I defend myself for keeping this secret, even though I know it was wrong.

"If I had realized it was that bad, I would have gone to Sam myself," Leo says. And I know he would have. I didn't want to draw that kind of attention to myself, so I kept most of it from him.

"I should have been honest about it, but I didn't want to start a feud between you guys and the Sheridans. It was stupid to keep it secret, though. I realize that now. I promise, I won't hide anything else from you guys," I insist, knowing that my apology is pointless.

I can't help feeling like I've broken their trust, and wondering how long it will take to repair, if it's even possible. Remy must sense my fear, because he pulls me into his arms. "Hanna, I know you think you were protecting my brothers.

But putting yourself at risk isn't worth it. We're not mad at you. I understand why you hid this. Just don't do it again. We want you to be safe." He presses a kiss to my forehead, and I close my eyes to hold back the tears.

Will comes back into the room. "Sam's gonna come back in a bit to talk to you about what you told us, Hanna. I need Leo and Remy to help me put the plywood up now that the cops are done with the living room. Do you want to wait for us here, or come outside with us?"

His concern is touching, but I'm not sure what I need right now. "Would it be okay if I took a bath while you guys take care of the windows? I can clean up the glass inside first," I offer.

Remy shakes his head. "You go take a bath. We'll clean up and take care of the windows. Focus on relaxing; maybe listen to one of your books and use the bubbles Leo got for you."

Each of my guys kisses me, then I'm ushered toward the stairs. I can't believe how lucky I got with this pack. I'd started to think I would never have this, then Remy came back. Part of me is still mad at him for leaving in the first place, but I understand why he felt like he had to. We really need to start trusting each other and communicating better.

I gather my fluffy bathrobe and the new towels my Alpha bought for me, then head to my bathroom. Starting the water, I add some of the buttercup and berry scented bubble bath Leo surprised me with last week. The sweet, musky scent fills the room while I get everything ready.

Darting back into my nest, I grab my e-reader and ear buds. I can't help thinking about the last bath I took while trying to listen to a book. Hopefully this one doesn't end with me losing my home. I shudder at the reminder of the fire that took the house I grew up in.

Slipping into the tub, I start my audiobook and put my e-reader on the counter beside the tub, out of the way.

LEO

"I can't believe you didn't tell us that she was being stalked," Remy says as we hold the plywood over the window for Will to attach it to the house.

"She didn't tell me until after it had stopped. And I had no idea it was one of the Sheridan boys," I argue. It's not like I kept it a secret. There was nothing I could do by the time I found out, especially when Hanna made it sound like whoever it was had left town.

"You two need to stop. It doesn't matter now. Sam will be here in a while, and he'll figure out what needs to happen next. We can't be fighting each other when he gets here. That's what they want. To push our pack apart. Somehow, they think they can take Hanna from us if they split us up. We can't let that happen," Will insists. And he's right.

We finish hanging the plywood over the broken windows, then head inside to clean up while Hanna takes her bath. Remy grabs the broom and dustpan while Will puts his tools away.

I drag the trash can into the living room and help my older brother clean up the glass. "We'll probably have to vacuum too, but we'll get most of it this way," he says as he sweeps the furniture and floor.

Cleaning up doesn't take long when Will joins us. The three of us have the living room back in order before Hanna comes downstairs from her bath. She's wrapped up in one of my hoodies with a pair of flannel pajama pants and fuzzy socks. Her dark hair is pulled up in a messy bun. I fight the urge to take it down and run my fingers through it.

A knock at the door makes everyone jump. Will laughs and walks over to answer it. "We don't have to hang out in this room if you aren't comfortable," I say to Hanna when Will leads Sam back into the living room.

"You guys got that all cleaned up fast," Sam says, gesturing to the living room.

"I'm okay. We can talk here. This isn't going to be a comfortable conversation anyway," she answers, taking a seat on the couch. Sam sits in the chair across from her.

"Will tells me you have some things to share," Sam starts. "And I can't help wondering why you didn't come to me sooner." His disappointment is evident, and Hanna shrinks in on herself for a minute.

"Sam," Remy warns. That one word is all it takes for Hanna to realize that we're not going to let him berate her for not talking.

twenty-one

You're Safe Now

HANNA

My face flushes at Remy's rebuke of Sam. "It's okay, Rem. I should have said something sooner. Things might not have gotten this bad if I had."

"I don't care. No one is going to guilt you about this. We've done enough of that, and you don't deserve it," he argues. I can tell that he's not going to let me apologize for my part in this.

I turn to Sam, recounting my story again. He stops me to ask a few questions, and I realize that he's gathering information to use when he questions Jesse. "I'll have to see if I can get witness statements. This won't be easy to prove if he doesn't confess, since you didn't keep the notes or gifts." Before I can respond, Sam holds up a hand. "I understand why you didn't keep them, and I'm not saying you should have. It just makes our case harder to prove. I want you to know, I believe you. And other people will, too. That won't get us very far with the courts, though."

"I understand," I say quietly. I want to crawl in a hole and give up. But doing that will allow not only Jesse to get away with what he did, but also would give Bo a free pass with his lies. And since their cousin is coming forward, maybe she'll know about what Jesse did, too. "Do you think Katie knows anything about what Jesse did?"

Sam hums as he considers my question. My guys stare at him, waiting for his answer. "It's definitely possible. I'll stop by the hospital and ask her on my way home. They'll probably argue that you guys intimidated her somehow to make her turn against them. But we've got a protective detail stationed outside her room, and she hasn't changed her story at all since she woke up. It helps that the first thing she did when she woke up was to ask if Leo was okay."

After a few more questions, Sam thanks us for our time and leaves. He promises to call if there's anything else he needs. We should hear something in a day or so. Apparently, I'll have to meet with a lawyer and press charges for stalking for this to go anywhere. I'm not looking forward to that, but if it protects my pack, that's what I'll do.

Once we're alone again, Remy pulls me into his arms and presses a kiss to my forehead. "I'm proud of you."

"For what? Hiding things and escalating a situation that could have already been handled?" I respond.

Leo steps up behind me, sandwiching me between them. "For telling the truth, even though it was hard." His kind words embarrass me, and I duck my head against Remy's chest.

"Okay, fuck off, you two. It's my turn to hold our Omega," Will insists, shoving at his brothers. It's playful and lighthearted, making Remy and Leo laugh. For a minute, I think they'll tease him by keeping me away, but then I'm pushed into his arms.

Will captures my mouth with his, kissing me like a starving man having his last meal. I can't help scenting the room, maple and cinnamon surround us as slick pools in my panties. Through our bond, I can feel what my scent does to each of them. Before I know what's happening, I'm tossed over Will's shoulder and carried to my nest. I squeal at the sudden movement, laughing when Leo and Remy follow us.

WILL

With everything that's happened in the past twenty-four hours, I know Hanna could use a distraction. Not only that, but we need to connect as a pack. Our Omega doesn't feel safe, and she's worried about us. Some quality time in the nest will help ease those fears.

"Will! Put me down!" she squeals as I carry her up the stairs.

I ignore her pleas until we're inside the nest. Leo closes the door behind us once all four of us are inside. I ease Hanna to her feet. "I understand how you're feeling right now. And yes, we have things we need to discuss, but you also need to feel safe while we do that. This is the most secure room in the house," I explain, resting my hands on her hips. I press a kiss to her temple, then drag her down on the inset mattress with me.

Hanna burrows into a pile of pillows and blankets, then does grabby hands at us because she wants us to crawl in around her. Of course, we do what she wants, snuggling in as close as we can.

"I've already arranged for the windows to be replaced to-morrow. And a security company is coming to put in an alarm system, complete with perimeter cameras and a doorbell cam," Remy says, once we're all settled in.

"I think those are great ideas," Leo agrees. I nod, none of this being news to me. I expected him to go more overboard than he is.

"Now that I know everything is taken care of, can we watch a movie and snuggle?" Hanna asks. I'm relieved that she's not afraid to tell us what she needs. I'd been concerned that she would use what's happening to pull away from us.

"Absolutely. Do you want me to text Mandi and see if they can open tomorrow?" Remy asks, getting up to grab the remote and some movie snacks. Hanna nods, wiping tears from her cheeks.

With everything settled, Remy hands Leo the remote, and he finds Hanna's favorite movie. The four of us snuggle deeper into the plush softness of Hanna's nest. She rests her head on my chest, and before the movie is half-way over, she's snoring softly.

"She was exhausted," Leo says with a yawn.

"We all are," I agree. "Sleep is the best thing for all of us tonight. We've got a lot to deal with tomorrow."

"Exactly. We have to be ready for anything," Remy insists. With a basic plan in place, or rather an agreement that we need a plan, we all fall asleep with Hanna in the middle of the nest.

REMY

I wake to my phone ringing. "What time is it?" Hanna mutters, snuggling closer.

A glance at my phone has me swearing. "Fuck. It's early; go back to sleep. I have to take this," I answer, easing her onto Leo so I can answer the call. I rush out of the nest and slide my finger along the screen.

"What's wrong, Sam?" I ask, wondering if he can hear my racing heart through the phone.

"Bo made a full confession once he found out that Katie told us everything. And we're still searching for Jesse. Looks like he might have skipped town, along with the old man. Lucas swears he has no idea where they are. We've got a manhunt going, and you have my word we will do everything we can to keep your pack safe," Sam assures me.

"Well, if Bo confessed, that's a good thing, right? I doubt Jesse or his grandfather will come back if they know that Katie and Bo have told you everything. Were you able to confirm the stalking?" I can't stop myself from asking the question. Hanna needs to know.

"Between Bo's, Katie's, and Lucas' statements, we were. Each of them witnessed part of what Hanna told us. If we find Jesse and his grandfather, they'll both be going away for a long time. It turns out that the old man was more involved in everything that we realized. He convinced Bo and Jesse that they had a claim on Hanna, and urged them to take what they wanted. When he couldn't brainwash Lucas, he started ignoring him," Sam explains.

I scrub a hand over my face, relief washing over me. This isn't over by any means, but I feel safer knowing that the cops are on our side. "Thanks, Sam. I'll make sure Hanna knows. We're getting the new windows today, and the security system with cameras. So, we'll have video evidence if anything else happens."

"Perfect. I'll swing by later to see how it's coming along and make sure everyone is doing okay. Do you need me to bring anything?" he asks.

"You could bring your girl over for a visit with ours," I tease, wondering if he realizes that everyone knows he's in love with Maisy.

He scoffs. "What? I don't have a girl," he claims.

"Not even a petite little redhead? Okay. Well, I'll give her a call and see if she wants to spend some time with Hanna, then." I pause, waiting for him to take the bait.

A deep sigh echoes through the line. "I'll bring her with me."

"Don't worry about it, Sam. We're not telling anyone. Y'all will work it out, I'm sure," I offer.

"Thanks, man. We're trying to get Ed to agree to let us court her, but her brother Aaron is our biggest roadblock. He and Joey don't get along, and it makes things difficult."

"You'll figure it out, I'm sure. Look at us. I mean, Hanna is still pissed at me, but she's ours now. You guys can get there. Maisy won't let her dad say no forever," I offer. After a few more words of encouragement, I disconnect the call and get ready for the window guys and the security installation. I plan to let everyone else sleep as long as possible. The past couple of days have been miserable, and I know we all want to put it behind us.

LEO

When Remy doesn't immediately come back upstairs, I relax and hold Hanna for a while. She's restless, and before long, ends up curled into Will's side. I take that chance to get up and moving for the day. After a quick shower in my room, I throw on a pair of sweats and head downstairs to make breakfast.

Since we're not going anywhere today, I'm hoping I can talk Remy into making something a little fancy for dinner tonight. If he's not up for cooking, though, we'll just order pizza and take it easy. When I get to the kitchen, I see the window replacement crew is already working. Remy has made coffee, and is putting a batch of muffins in the oven.

"I didn't expect you to make breakfast," I admit.

"It's Hanna's orange cranberry muffin recipe. I thought she might like them this morning," he replies with a shrug. I can't get over how much he's opening up since we finally claimed our Omega.

"You're a good Alpha," I tell him, pouring a cup of coffee and taking a seat at the table.

"I could be better," he argues. "If I hadn't run off before, none of this would be happening."

I shake my head. Before I can respond, I hear Hanna's voice behind me. "You can't know that. This could have all happened no matter what you did before. And blaming yourself is cruel. If anything, it's my fault for not going to Sam when Jesse started harassing me."

I turn in time to see Will pull her into his arms. "That's not fair and you know it. No one is to blame here except the family who tried to separate us. The Sheridans did all of this. It's not Remy's fault or yours. And I'm not letting any of you wallow in guilt over it."

"I agree with Will. All we can do now is move forward. That starts with the new windows and the security system. Looks like both of which are well underway now. So, we lean on each other, and do what we have to in order to protect our pack," I insist.

We know there's a chance that this isn't over, and we'll be prepared for it. But not at the cost of living our lives and being happy. I refuse to let that happen. I may not be an Alpha, but I'm prepared to fight like one if I have to.

HANNA

The next few days are a blur. The window installation is quick, but the security system takes two full days to get situated. Then we have to learn how to use it. I'm convinced that Sam is going to stop answering the alarm calls after the fifth time Remy manages to set it off accidentally. But none of the responding officers get angry. They seem to understand the situation and that gets to me. On one hand, they understand the danger we're facing, which is comforting and terrifying. On the other, they're determined to protect my pack from any harm.

"I'm sorry, Sam. If it's any consolation, this time it was Leo who set it off, not me," Remy says when Sam knocks on the door.

"No worries. I'm happy to stop by as many times as it takes to make sure y'all are safe," he answers. Remy steps out of the way for Sam to enter the house and search it.

The whole thing seems silly to me, but Sam insists every time that he just wants to make sure we're okay. "You know this isn't necessary, Sam," Leo insists.

Sam holds a finger to his mouth, and I wonder if he's heard something. A chill runs up my spine, and I step closer to Remy. He wraps his arms around me as if he's concerned too. I sense his worry along our bond. When I start to ask him about it, he shakes his head slightly.

My heart races, pulse pounding in my ears. Sam moves from room to room quickly, silently. I barely breathe while he searches our home for intruders. I want to protest when Will follows Sam up the stairs, but Remy holds me tighter and shares a look with Leo.

I can almost hear their unspoken exchange. *Maybe it wasn't Leo who set off the alarm this time.* That thought terrifies me. I mean, I've gotten used to one of us setting the alarm off accidentally, then laughing about our tech problems. But if someone is inside the house, that's different.

Will's shock zaps me along our bond before I hear his growl. Remy pushes me into Leo's arms and races upstairs. "Wait," I cry, unable to stop myself.

"It's okay. Sam is with them. We're gonna hide until they come get us," Leo says, pulling me toward the laundry room. I guess I didn't catch the entire exchange between him and Remy, after all. I let him drag me into the small room, where he barricades the door with his body and holds me against him. "We'll be safe here."

My body shakes as fear takes hold. I find myself terrified that Will and Remy are hurt; that somehow whoever broke in has overpowered Sam. There's nothing I can do to help them. I lock eyes with Leo when I hear the fighting start. Someone falls down the stairs, then a gunshot echoes through the house.

Leo wraps his arms around me tighter, as if holding me closer will save me from the horror of my imagination. I scream when the door rattles behind him. This is it; we're done. I can't help thinking about all the things I never got to do, and regretting the time I spent angry with Remy over stupid things. If only we had more time. I would do better.

"Leo, open the door. Sam got him," Remy calls out. My eyes go wide, and I step out of Leo's embrace. He opens the door slowly, as if he's not sure it's really Remy letting us know it's okay.

With the door open, I can see Remy with a split lip and Will sporting a black eye. But they're alive. I race out the door, throwing myself at them. I can't speak past the tears as I hug them both tightly and let myself break down.

Remy rubs my back and Will kisses my temple. "It's okay, cupcake." The words are reassuring and their scents calm me.

"Wilson took him to the station. I understand that you may not see it this way, but honestly, that was the best thing that could have happened. We've got him on breaking and entering, which will help the stalking charges stick," Sam says as if I have any idea what he's talking about.

"It was Jesse?" Leo asks, and I feel as if a light comes on, suddenly understanding what's happening here.

Sam nods. "He got a couple of good hits in on Remy and Will before they managed to shove him down the stairs. I shot him in the leg so he couldn't run off. But we got him. We'll be investigating Lucas too, just to be sure that you won't have any more trouble. I think you're safe now."

I don't know how to react to those words. *You're safe now.* There was a time when not being safe would have seemed strange. But with the past few days, everything feels a little surreal.

"Thanks, Sam. We appreciate everything you and the guys have done for us," Remy says, shaking Sam's hand. I know that we'll probably have to go down to the station later to answer questions and help finalize reports or something, but right now, I'm just processing the fact that we're safe.

Both Jesse and Bo are in custody. Neither of them will be coming after any of us again. It's a little ridiculous how comforting that thought is to me. I hadn't even realized how big a threat either of them was until Bo kidnapped Leo. Fuck, this has been a long week.

After Sam leaves, Will resets the alarm. It seems silly, but I feel safer with it on. "Do you think that the first few accidental set offs were Jesse testing the system?" he asks Remy.

Our Alpha shrugs. "Could have been, but I doubt he'll tell us if we ask," Remy answers.

Epilogue

HANNA

With the chaos caused by the Sheridan family behind us, moving forward is easy. Or as easy as anything can be when Remy Kerrisk is involved. He's still a pain in my ass, even now. But the past two years have been a learning experience for all of us. Evans' Bakery has officially expanded to include catering and lunch service. In addition to that, Leo's Place serves dinner now—thanks to Remy and his diner recipe tweaks.

It took longer than I would have liked, but we've managed to come together as a pack. Wiping the sweat from my brow, I turn to the cupcakes I've been working on this morning. I cannot think of a better way to let my guys know that our family is expanding than with custom baked goods.

Since today is Remy's day off, I'm able to pull this surprise off without getting caught. Will is working on commissions, and Leo is at the bar until this evening. Keeping this secret has been the most difficult thing I've ever had to do, but seeing their surprise will be worth it.

"You're telling them tonight, right?" Maisy asks, popping into the kitchen.

I laugh as I pipe icing onto a cupcake. "That is the plan, unless you spoil the surprise before then," I tease.

Rissa grabs a cupcake and bites into it. "Hey! Those are not for you!" I scold her. I'm glad my friends are spending more time with me lately. I'll need their support for this new chapter of my life.

"If you didn't want us to know, you should have done a better job of keeping a secret," she laughs.

I shake my head at her, and finish the cupcakes. "Help me box these up so I can get home."

Maisy grabs a box, and Rissa starts loading cupcakes into it. "How many of these are you taking?"

"One dozen for us, one for each of you to share with your guys," I answer with a grin. "Did you really think I wasn't going to share?"

The three of us dissolve into giggles after packing up all the cupcakes. The box I've specially decorated for my guys is set aside, and the girls help me finish cleaning up the bakery to close for the day. Once we're finished, Maisy drives me home.

Remy meets me at the door, taking the box from me. "I was coming to pick you up in a bit. Is everything okay?" He eyes the box suspiciously.

"The girls helped me clean up, and Mais offered to drive me home. I made dessert for tonight," I answer, avoiding his question. It won't do to spill the beans now, since I'm trying to surprise them. I wonder if he suspects anything, but want to avoid drawing extra suspicion if he doesn't. "When are Will and Leo gonna be home?"

He sets the box on the counter and turns back to me. "An hour or so, I think," he says, stepping closer and caging me against the opposite counter. "Plenty of time for me to make you glad you came home early."

Without warning, I find myself tossed over Remy's shoulder and being carried upstairs to my nest. My laughter fills the air, along with my cinnamon maple scent. Does it smell different now? Will he just know? I push those thoughts away and focus on the Alpha who is currently sliding me down his hard body to drop me on the inset mattress in the center of my nest.

I pull him on top of me, crashing my lips to his in a desperate kiss. How did I think I could survive without this Alpha? His kiss, his touch, his knot...he's everything I need. Along with his brothers, Remy is perfect for me.

When he breaks the kiss, we're both panting. Remy strokes his hands down my body, and I fight back a shiver. "You look tired, love. Are you sure that you're okay?" The tender question nearly breaks me. I'm dying to tell him, but want to wait for the pack to all be here.

"I'm fine. I promise," I say, sliding my hand into his hair to pull him back to my mouth. The kiss is needy and passionate, just like me. I want him, but I need to slow this down. If I'm not careful, I will let my secret slip in the heat of things.

Remy narrows his eyes at me as he pulls away again. "I don't buy it. You need to rest. We all know that you haven't been sleeping well," he argues. Is he trying to start a fight with me right now? What the hell just happened?

"Okay, I'm a little tired. But it's no big deal," I counter.

"It is a big deal to us," he says. "You need to take better care of yourself."

His concern is touching, but I'm not sure what changed all of a sudden to make him angry. "Remy, what's wrong?" I ask.

"They're getting out tomorrow." Oh, that. Yeah, I'd been trying to avoid this conversation for days. I know that Bo and Jesse are going to be released soon, but I don't want to think about it. The nightmares are back, but more out of concern for the life I'm nurturing inside of me than worry for my pack.

"Tomorrow? Wow, I didn't realize it was that soon," I say. It doesn't matter that I knew it was this week or next. He's going to blame the sleepless nights on that. And he's not completely wrong.

"We're going to protect you, cupcake," he vows.

I cup his cheek with my hand. "I know you will." We've changed so much of how we live since all of this started. It's rare for any of us to be alone unless we're home with the security system engaged. I can't help worrying that it will get worse with my news and the Sheridans' release.

REMY

I can tell that Hanna is hiding something from me. I'm just not sure what it is. I'd thought she was upset about the Sheridans' upcoming release from jail, but that doesn't seem to be it. Or not all of it anyway.

What else could it be? I know she hasn't been sleeping well this week, and I'm starting to worry. "Are you sure there's not something else?" I don't want to pressure her or fight, but my concern takes over.

"I'm fine, Remy. Just tired. Could we snuggle for a bit and have a nap before Leo and Will come home?" I can tell she's at least a little disappointed that I went from kissing to interrogating. I just can't shake off the feeling that there's something she's not telling me.

I nod at her request and pull her onto my chest, settling back onto her pillows in the nest. Sleep doesn't come easily for her, but I won't give up. I rub my hand up and down her back until she relaxes and her breath levels out.

A few minutes after she's out, I join her, letting go of my worry and drifting off to sleep.

LEO

I wipe down the bar, wondering if today will be the day that Hanna tells us what's been bothering her. I know that Remy is convinced she's worried about the Sheridan boys getting out of jail, but I don't think that's it.

I actually think she has good news to tell us, but I won't let myself say it out loud, not even in my own mind. Once Jasper takes over at Leo's place, I drive over and pick Will up.

"I can't wait to see Hanna today," he says.

"I think we're all anxious to see what she says," I admit.

My brothers and I are planning to take her away for a few days, just to be sure she feels safe with her tormentors being released. I don't think she'll agree to it, but Remy insisted that we plan a weekend getaway.

The smell of pasta sauce wafts at us as we enter the house. My mouth waters and I follow the smell to the kitchen. The box of cupcakes on the counter seems out of place, but I don't give them much attention.

"You guys set the table. Hanna is taking a shower before dinner. Apparently, she has something important to talk to us about. I couldn't get anything else out of her about it," Remy says.

"Is that why she brought cupcakes home?" Will asks, reaching for the box.

"Don't you dare," she growls from the doorway. Will turns, his eyes wide. "Those are for after dinner." The stern tone is not something we hear from Hanna, and it catches us all off guard.

"I'm sorry," he says, holding up his hands in surrender. Will and I rush off to set the table.

HANNA

I know I've overreacted here, but I can't take it back. If Will had opened that box, my secret would be out. And I'm not ready yet.

"Is dinner ready?" I ask Remy, keeping an eye on the box of cupcakes as if one of my guys is going to burst into the room and run off with it.

"Almost. They're setting the table, then we'll be ready to eat. You wanna grab the salad?" he asks, gesturing to the fridge.

I carry the salad to the table, then go back for the dressing and finally carry the box of cupcakes in as well. Remy puts the bowl of spaghetti in the center of the table, along with the fresh garlic bread.

"I thought the cupcakes were for later," Leo says with a smirk.

"They're for whenever I decide to let you guys have them," I answer, glaring at him for a second before shaking my head and laughing. "I want to make you wait, but I just don't have the patience for it."

With the three of them here, I'm anxious to tell them. We all take our seats and Leo serves drinks around the table. Remy fills plates with spaghetti and bread. Then I can't wait any longer.

"I have something I need to tell you," I say, standing up and grabbing the cupcake box. I pop it open, dropping a special cupcake in front of each of my guys.

They look down at the baked goods, then back up at me. No one speaks, and I start to wonder if this was a good idea. "Someone say something," I whisper. My heart races and sweat trickles down my spine. Surely, they're not upset, right? This is good news. Or is it?

"Buttercup, does this mean what I think it does?" Leo asks, holding the cupcake up and pointing at it.

I smile. "What if it does?" I ask, knowing that teasing is not the best idea. I just can't help it.

"Hanna," Remy breathes.

"You're pregnant?!" Will shouts, then shoves the whole cupcake in his mouth at my laugh.

"I need to know how you guys feel about this. You're scaring me a little," I admit.

Leo smiles at me, but Remy moves faster than either of his brothers. He grabs me, hugging tightly and pressing a kiss to my temple. "I can't speak for them, but I am thrilled," he says into my ear. "I can't wait to worship you and show just how excited I am for this."

My core twitches at his words, and I feel slick soaking my panties. Relief washes over me, and I let myself be passed from one brother to another while they tell me how exciting and awesome this is. At some point, my stomach growls loudly, and they decide we need to actually eat.

I'm pulled onto Will's lap, where he feeds me spaghetti and bread as if I'm an invalid who can't care for herself. The joy in his eyes is enough to keep me there. I know that these men will take care of me, and keep our children safe.

Between bites, I answer all of their questions about my pregnancy. I'm not sure what I expected, but it was not this level of interest. All three of them are completely involved, declaring that they will take care of me each step of the way.

And with everything we've been through, I know that they mean it. These men, my Alphas and Beta, will protect and care for me forever. We'll never be torn apart again, and that thought makes my heart smile.

The Story Continues...

Keep an eye out for news about the next two books in this series, Maisy and Karissa, by following my social media!

You can find all my links on: https://www.mpstarkweather.com

About the Author

M.P. Starkweather is a wife, mother, author, poet, casual online gamer, self-proclaimed fan-girl, and full-time nerd. She writes free-form poetry, paranormal romance, sci-fi romance, reverse harem romance, omegaverse romance, and is branching out into contemporary romance. In her free time, she enjoys writing, reading, Dungeons & Dragons, table top games with her husband and friends, and playing with her son. M.P. also enjoys tv, movies, and music across various genres.

To get the most up-to-date information about her latest releases and book signings, check out www.mpstarkweather.com or follow her on your favorite social media site.

Also By M.P. Starkweather

Standalones – Contemporary RH

<u>Finding Fiona</u>

Standalones - Contemporary RH OV

<u>Forsaken Omega</u> – free with newsletter signup

<u>Cold Princes</u>

<u>Knot My Valentine</u>

Omegas of Echo Falls – Contemporary RH OV series

<u>Hanna</u>
Maisy
Karissa

The Pack Next Door – Contemporary RH OV series

<u>Princess or Knot</u>

<u>Fiancée or Knot</u>

<u>Queen or Knot</u>

<u>The Pack Next Door: The Original Trilogy</u>

<u>Christmas or Knot</u>

Standalones – Paranormal RH

<u>The Wayward Girl</u>

The Cursed Blade Series – Paranormal w/ different pairings

<u>Digital Blade</u> – RH
<u>Elemental Blade</u> – RH

Vampires at Midnight - Paranormal RH series
<u>Blood Moon</u>

<u>Blood Lost</u>

<u>Blood War</u>

<u>Vampires at Midnight: The Complete Trilogy</u>

VaM/HoF Crossover Novella - Paranormal RH

Blood Wolf— free with newsletter signup

Hunters of the Forest - Paranormal RH series

Wolf Bane

Wolf Caged

Wolf Moon

Hunters of the Forest: The Complete Trilogy

Forged by Magic - Sci-fi/Fantasy M/F series

Hidden

Betrayed

Saved

Forged by Magic: The Complete Trilogy

Daydreams and Sunsets - a collection of poetry

Daydreams and Sunsets